Heaven In Las Vegas

Sherman Henry Smith Jr

DEDICATION

This novel is dedicated to Sherman Jaelen Smith.

CONTENTS

PROLOGUE

It's amazing what a man can do after he realizes that all of the hard work he did in order to get to where he is at was all in vain, because eventually he's going to die anyway. Sure, it's a darkening philosophy, if it could be called that, however the means to which a person goes to find something that they seek is their desire for that something. When you realize that everything ends as it begins, swiftly, you gain an appreciation for what you have and even for what was once and is no more. Many times I've sat and wondered how a person could let their life slip away from them; let their inner dream and desire for what they truly want flee from them as a playful toddler does her mother. It must be a pain in the ass to go through life with a bunch of woulda's and coulda's, especially as an old man with nothing else to live for other than what they are sitting in front of at that very moment. Old men become content with what they have because they have spent much of their time rejecting what their soul has told them to do. They were fine with living in a world that someone else created, this someone not having the man's best interest at heart, because it isn't their heart that they are leading.

I have come to learn that people will accept you and love you for you, as long as you that they love are what they want you to be. They become a part of you, and you of them, yet they want to change you. Sure, they may say that they love you, but if you do not change in the way that they feel you should then they become upset with who they have chosen to love. This type of possession is deadly because it kills the spirit of the one who is to be changed. Love, as it lies in the depths of everything and every person is not a possessive emotion. In fact, it is not an emotion at all. Love is energy. It cannot be created or destroyed. It can only be transferred from one thing to the next. I often wonder about love and what it actually is made of. It must be pure matter because the truth of love is one that never spoils and will never go away. Love is perfect, however often times I think of love as an imperfection. This imperfection, like a mole on your face or a scar below your eye, is something that you must grow to love and appreciate through time. You learn its behaviors and what is inside of it to make it what it is. You embrace it, but not before you learn to cover it and how to stand as to not draw attention to it. Initially, it is something that is deplorable to you. You hate it and want so badly to do away with it. Is this feeling love? Maybe in the grand scheme of things as time has run its course, you have grown to appreciate and love an imperfection as what it truly is; perfect. Maybe it is the case that time is what makes a bond stronger. Yet, I am becoming against this notion and everything that I thought I knew more and more each day. Love cannot be a possession. It must not. You shouldn't have to grow into love. One should love what they are and who they are and everything about themselves, in order to love everything else. This is why I believe that the true love, one that is of the highest energy and frequency, is from the soul. And from the soul one can reach into the universe and the power of God. When you love a person, you obsess over being separated. Our attention is submersed in the substance of what isn't there. You obsess over a void. Once you are with them again, you wish that their face would stop looking at you. If that is love then that is a load of shit, so I understand why people are heartless. The best part about being heartless is that you don't have to worry about coronary disease. This may be dandy to you pricks, but I am far too fascinated by what manages to bind all of us completely different people together. That force that binds us is love. I am not searching for it, yet I am fascinated by it, because it is all around. It is the force that allows people to touch even when they are not anywhere near each other. When lovers are oceans apart, one may blow a kiss in the wind and it may reach his woman, or an ocean breeze may carry her perfume into his nose from miles away. It must be a remarkable feeling. Even more so when one has never known love and meets it for the first time. Love at first sight? Sure. But love at first smile or first smell or first touch is much more intuitive and connective, because that feeling is one that fills that void. When you meet them you know you loved them before you met them. When you met them you knew you loved them before you knew they existed.

I believe wholeheartedly that we often force ourselves into becoming parts of people because we don't listen to ourselves. So, our souls, hearts, self's; they become more quiet as time goes on. Everything is one and when we learn the unwritten language of the universe...one that words cannot understand; we find our own path. There has to be a duality to everything, a life and a death, a design and a purpose, a use and a destiny. Our soul won't respond to us anymore because it doesn't want to get hurt. It knows you won't do what you're supposed, so it doesn't tell you. And that is why our souls stop talking to us, because it knows that our words will defeat it. When I came to recognize that love is what binds us all together, I stopped wanting a need for validation from others because everyone else's need is just as transparent. There is no better feeling than having to go through something that had to happen in order to reach a point that was once thought unattainable, which is why I find myself where I am today. I got tired of living in you all's world and I decided to create my own. If I never would have entered into the bottom of yours, I would not cherish the top of my own. I feel the wonder in my world and I hold onto it tightly. There is nothing that cannot be done and nothing that is limited, because it is my world and I have an abundance of everything. The universe and the unseen are at my disposal and through rampant drug use and meditation I have learned to harness this power, within a society where "nothing is new" is the determining factor in drug usage having a profound effect on a person's life...but in this day and age, what is excess? Is it all a personal experience or is there a threshold that no one should cross? Drugs once thought as relics are returning and where uppers and downers are a way of life, one must contend with his own vices while demonstrating care over others. It is quite a dual experience. Many people understand drugs and the powers that they hold, both positive and negative. Excess? Why are the people who cross this threshold the only ones who know where it is? People have billions upon billions of dollars and have never-ending sex. People indulge in the most delectable foods and merchandise that life can offer. Is their excess any more different than mine? Why is it looked down upon to smoke an immense amount of marijuana and not looked down upon to buy innumerable cars? Just like there are different cars, there are different strains of marijuana.

I understand the wife of the city Mayor that began her journey as a high school cheerleader who enjoyed prescription pills and turned into a 40-year old addicted to pain killers. I understand her husband's strife in having to deal with the wife who ventured into heroin use when pills stopped working. Just as well, I understand the wealthy man who has divorced 4 wives in his lifetime due to "irreconcilable differences". He sought love and they sought his wealth. I understand why he now only deals with high-priced escorts and engages in extravagant weekends with enough MDMA and cocaine to keep a Rhinoceros awake for a month. I understand the high school kid who experimented with promethazine-codeine syrup so much that he became addicted and, wanting a relief from the pain of going through opiate withdrawal, became consumed with ecstasy usage. From ecstasy in high-school to acid and DMT in college, the excess of his usage brought him an excess in power of the mind. So much so that he went on to harness the power of the God particle and transformed his life into an experiment with alchemy. The only issue I have is time and I realize that patience is the pinnacle of my success, for the things I visualize are already done, I must only wait for them to materialize on this plane. The only problem I foresee for myself is that many artists and philosophers have had idealistic and spiritual breakthroughs only to end up sizzling away into reclusiveness, dying at a young age, or driven to utter insanity.

Once you finally give in to the weirdness and idiocy of what in the hell you're doing and ride the wave into oblivion, it can go one of two ways. The first way is into a maniacal stupor, equipped with harsh words and harsh tactics for the sole reason of destroying yourself or the poor sap who decided to be your baby sitter for the night while you tripped out on LSD and cocaine with a fifth of Bombay Sapphire, causing you to forget everything in the world that you once knew about life. This could lead to prison, or death depending on how crazed the lunatic in your subconscious that's been lying in wait, ready to destroy you, is. The other way is much more pleasant, but frightening as well. By the way, I've never tried LSD, although I read an AP story in the Courier-Journal about a man who bugged out on acid and ate his girlfriend's heart. All the better I suppose, in the grand scheme of things. She may have been a mass murderer, or even worse…a double agent sent from the rival university. The poor guy was a football player, a humongous puppy that didn't want anything more than to love and cherish small wildlife. He even taught kids how to play the cello at the local orphanage. And this rat, the spy from the cross state rival, some four hundred miles away firmly comes along from a decrepit mess of a school, the rival university. Douches in sweater vests and oxford button down tee-shirts, their khaki slacks pinned tightly to their waists. Everyone knows the school song and on Wednesdays the debate team does a chili give away during the cold months. Real classy...She got with the nincompoop simply to steal the playbook. It was the rival coach's daughter. If I weren't Christian, I'd curse the ground. On second thought, the guy was kind of sinister. He's the first outcome.

The second is to allow the wave of incredible uncertainty to force the expansion of your consciousness. It can be had in a multitude of ways and its name is all the description of it that a mildly intelligent person would need to be able to conceptualize. But for you dopes, it is when you force your own conscious to expand. When you take that ride into the unknown, knowing that a line must be crossed but being uncertain as to how it is going to end...As a child is on Christmas, you'll go to sleep with the uncertainty of what you will receive, and once you awaken you will be happy or disappointed. Don't be disappointed. Buy, and ride the wave into a place that you did not know existed. Understanding that one is a limitless machine, all you need to do is figure out the level of risk involved. There is no better feeling than running through a wall to the other side of something. It had to happen. It was challenging but the rewards were profound.

TUESDAY, 5:08 A.M. EST

I remember when I lost it all. There was something so special about that place. Staring into the moonlight at 4:30 a.m. drunk off of Gin and buzzed to Pluto with cocaine and marijuana, you begin to wonder where your life took a turn for the worse. Sitting on a curb near an I-65 South expressway on-ramp in Downtown Louisville, Kentucky eating gas burgers may also have something to do with it, but that scenario can all be attributed to the booze.

"Where the fuck is my car again?" I slurred while miniature onions flew from my mouth.

Those damned onion-flavored cabbage shavings, I hate them. I had forgotten to tell them not to put them on my burger.

"Shit, over at the gas station parking lot. Remember, you parked to get some gas and we ended up walking to get food," Rob replied, stuffing a double cheeseburger into his mouth.

"You know bro, them ain't real onions. That's cabbage in onion juice." I had no idea where I had heard it, nor if it was true, but I kept telling it to people. Your mind kind of gets like that when you're intoxicated.

"Nah, you lying. I don't even like cabbage, but they good on this burger, so fuck it," Rob said as he grabbed his cellphone from his front pocket in order to call someone to pick us up and take us to my car. We could easily have walked to the car seeing that it was 500 feet away, but we figured it would be more fun to fuck with somebody at 5 in the morning.

~

We pulled up to Big Ted's after hour's spot. It's a decent place located above a restaurant that is members only, although now it's a fucking free-for-all. Still, there are rarely new faces. Standing outside of a large wooden door, Rob pressed a button that activated a camera that slowly turned towards us.

"Who the fuck is it?" a voice loomed from an intercom.

"Motherfucker you see us, it's me and Sherm."

After a buzz and loud click, we were up the stairs in a flash.

Upon entering the decrepit venue, you must purchase a

beverage, preferably alcoholic. Equipped with a pool table, flat screen television and leather seating, you have no choice but feel like you're in a 1990's R & B video. The poker tables in the back room were used for poker matches years ago, but now they are mostly used to break down cocaine.

"What up big dog!" I bellowed as I entered the door.

"Not shit man, where ya coming from?" Ted replied.

"The other side of the moon my good man, I made my own world and I'm living it up in this motherfucker."

"Well, that's good, Precious wants to know what you're drinking."

"Pass the Bombay! Add some OJ too," Rob interjected. "Say Ted, fucks gonna happen if I don't tip? I mean; you can't beat my ass."

"You're a stupid motherfucker. I'll shoot your fucking head off."

"Oh fuck you, fat boy. Here you go Precious, you know I was gonna tip you."

"Yeah, you'd better or else your black ass was gonna be eating .357 slugs for a late snack!" Ted roared, pulling a chrome.357 revolver from under his belly.

You see, Big Ted was cool. He had long hair and a horse shoe hairline, and came off as a smooth white guy. But by damn, he is one of those people that has absolutely no idea how to make a person feel safe, comfortable, or valuable. You cannot take the things he may say or do personal; it's just what it is. Luckily, we didn't give a fuck about anything with all the blow coursing through our bodies.

"Oh, you finally found a use for all them rolls huh motherfucker?" Rob said with a grin.

"Yeah bitch. Let's do some coke."

Ted was a motherfucker when it came to blow. He would set out line after line and with the sole window in the place covered by a black out curtain, before you know it its 1 p.m. and you've drank a pint of booze and snorted 12 lines off of a dirty wooden bar.

"This shit is the truth," Ted's voice boomed as he pulled his hand out of his pocket, holding a baggie of white rocks. Other patrons in the bar began to eye us, in wonderment at the commotion.

"What," screeched Rob. "Go back to playing pool! Get your

eyes the fuck on."

"Hey asshole," Ted playfully retorted, not bothering to look up. "This is my spot; I do the yelling."

"Fuck you Ted. Precious, I need another drink. Bourbon and Sprite, please."

I don't know about your personal philosophy, but in my unimportant opinion, every person resembles some type of animal. The funny thing is that this notion only exposes itself when I am high on blow. Not in the hallucinogenic way, but in a, damn you resemble a pug kind of way. And Precious really does resembles a pug! Man, it's quite comical when you think about it...her mushroom top haircut and face like a pug. Ha!

"Ok coming right up. Sherm, you want anything?" Precious said.

"No, I'm still working on this one I got. I'll take a bud light though."

I felt Rob's eyes on me. "Quit baby-sitting nigga! Yeah, give em another drink too!"

"See...this bastard. You're a horrible influence."

"Fuck you. Stop being a pussy, drink the fuck up," Rob said, a wide grin across his face.

By this time the bar-area had filled with people hoping to get in on the snow flake festivities. Being high, I took it upon myself to tap a man sitting next to me and begin small talk. Tonight, we are all friends in blow.

"Can you believe this fucker? I just got back from Atlanta on an interview with GCS Radio and this asshole has me loaded off of booze and powder. Shit!"

"Well shit, that's kind of journalistic man. The Freak would probably enjoy the fuck outta one of these night's."

That's when it hit me. Wow. Maybe this whole journalism - let's get loaded and experience and then write about it - shit may get me somewhere after all. The Freak was an extraordinary person with impeccable morals. And I would have loved to do a blotter with the old kook.

"What are you going to do down at GCS?" the man with no name asked.

"If I get the job I'll be writing news-stories and interviewing people...a ton of investigative bullshit."

"Well, good luck man. Car bomb on me," the no-named man

said, turning towards the bartender. "Precious, two car bombs!"

"Here we go motherfucker!" Rob's exclaimed, eyes glistening. As he sat, swiveling his head left and right, they continued to brighten and a smile the size of the St. Louis arch sprouted from the grin drawn across his face.

"What in the fuck are you so happy about? Act like you never seen any dope before." Ted didn't seem to thrilled at Rob's sudden rise in happiness.

Looking at Ted with an evil grin, Rob didn't speak, and instead let his action answer the question for him by whipping out the eight-ball of powder from earlier. I had no idea what the fuck he was so happy about; it wasn't like we had forgotten about it. Maybe he had however, but shit then again maybe not. When you're in a good mood and around good people, even devils will be relaxed and whimsical.

"We going haaaard tonight!" Rob yelled, ripping open the bag of already broken down powder, flinging it all over the bar counter. He eyed the strewn about powder for a few seconds, then took his finger and wiped it into a small mountain.

"Alright, who's first up? Sherm! Let's go nigga, it's Monday but you're leaving on Thursday for Vegas so you gotta prepare your body."

"Dude. I'm not going to cooperate with your evil," I responded, tooting the last of two lines laid out by Ted earlier in the night.

As Rob playfully toyed with his mound of booger sugar, Ted flippantly reacted.

"Look what you did asshole, you scooped the lines in. Give me a couple of those while you're over there messing in shit."

Laughing, Rob whipped out his driver' license and began separating the pile of snow into 30-inch-long lines, making the bar look like a pastry chef's work station. There was blow everywhere.

"Man I'm gonna have residue on my shit for days. Sherm, you say you interviewed in Atlanta. What you gonna be doing again?" Ted asked.

As I began to answer Ted's question, Precious decided to hand the no-name guy and I our Irish Car Bombs.

There's something sinister about these beverages that I'll never enjoy. Nothing good comes from this devilish concoction, only headaches and unhinged decisions. I can't waste a free drink however. The world over, free liquor can always be associated with good tithing. Bottoms up.

Slamming my glass down, I eyed Ted with a deathly stare that said 'I am dying slowly'.

"Writing the local news, mane," I smeared. My mouth was so numb that it was hard to speak. By this time, I was hit over my head drunk and high, but the more alcohol I drank the more coke I had to inhale. I've got to stay balanced. It's a fucking Monday for Christ-sake. And with me being a future Doctor of Communication, this may or may not be such a good way to handle myself.

~

I always find myself shifting between internal thought and reality, drifting between absent-mindedness and awareness. The alcohol brings about retardation while the cocaine clarifies everything I thought I knew as nothing more than conceited retardation. So, when I get in one of those introspective 'Oh my fucking God I am so fucking high and I am ruining my life' moments, I simply reiterate to myself that every hour is happy hour if you drown out the other emotions. Bad decisions make the most wonderful stories.

~

"Do women know they fucked up the world or nah?" I asked the room. No one answered, but their gazes coaxed me as if to say, 'carry on'.

"I mean shit, Eve, the mother of the earth was a damn hoe. The world's first. She did it in such great hoe-fashion too."

"Women are fucked up out here dog. That's why I do what I do," Rob chuckled, slapping fives with me.

"Yeah, that's why your ass is in a fucking love rectangle now. Ted, did this fool tell you what the fuck he did?"

"Nah, what did the motherfucker do?" Ted asked sarcastically.

"Damn Sherm, shit! Why you gotta tell his ass that?" Rob was vehement with his question. I could give a shit less if he was upset however. "Well look Ted, basically I got three girlfriends and they all know about each other and they are all crazy as fucking bats. Women are off!"

"Well ass hole, that's what you get."

We paused for a coke break, and each of us took a few lines from the table. I was the first one up, so I continued my story.

"Your love life sucks. Anyway…Eve goes and gets married. Then she gets seduced. And then she fucks the devil. Then she goes home like 'honey, look what I learned.' Fucking slut," I brought my nose down to the table and sniffed another line. "But that's not the worst thing. The devil is just laughing like 'haha I fucked his wife.'…Yeah he was laughing all right, until he got chopped down. Dumb ass devil, shouldn't have been bragging."

Everyone's now intent on listening to my story. I suppose the whole Eve is a hoe thing had gotten them reeled in. Or maybe they were interested because they were coked out of their minds. Either or, who cares…I'm in rare form.

"Eve done gave Adam a STD so he's trying to find something to cover the discharge with and God comes along like, 'bro what the fuck is this?'. Eve's ass tries to explain, but God's like 'shut your ass up and go bleed, Eve'. Then God is like, 'Adam bro, I told you don't trust that hoe but what did you do? You went and trusted her. Bro, you're crazy'. And by that time the devil is slithering around saying 'God bro! Look what I did bro. Dope, right?' Nigga! God was livid," I finished.

"Sherm, what does that have to do with anything?" Precious asked, a bewildered look on her face. I suppose being the only person not higher than giraffe pussy would make you wonder the going's on in my mind. Everyone else seemed to secretly understand.

"What I'm saying Precious is this," I replied, before taking a deep breath and sniffing a 6-inch line of coke. What the fuck am I thinking?

"…Holy shit!" Around this time my vision became very cloudy and I felt as if my body was going to throw itself off of the bar stool.

"Got damn man, what happened to today is Monday?" Rob couldn't believe that I had actually done that. I could only respond by tossing him an exasperated glance.

"The moral is this…" I continued. "I'll never be able to marry a chick because I'm going to assume that she got half nude pictures on the internet and somebody is gonna tweet me 'this yo wife or nah?'"

"Where in the fuck do you get this shit from?" laughed Rob, "You can't make this shit up. Who hurt you?"

"Fuck you." My head dropped and a situation that I had put in the back of my mind crept to its foreground and giggled at me. Why now?

"Bro, you got bitches."

He already knew what I was thinking about. Or rather, who I was thinking about. There are always times in a man's life when he reverts back to the primitive thinking of "worry" and there is no greater time for those thoughts to occur than when one has gotten out of a five-year relationship at the ripe old age of 25.

"You sound bitter."

"I am bitter."

Rob raised his eyebrows in surprise. I suppose he hadn't expected me to say that. But the fact was, that in that moment, I was bitter. I was still in love.

In that moment of thought, a feeling rose inside of me that caused such discomfort that I could do nothing but burst into uncontrollable laughter. The fit lasted for what seemed like 30 seconds, but could have been much longer. Oh, the things which humor you when you are in an altered state of mind...What the hell was I laughing about? You can't judge every book by its cover, but are women even books? Probably so, only because books and women require you to open and read them. Once I finally stopped laughing, "Don't judge a book by its cover. Unless that book is a fucking annoying prick that needs to be high-fived in the face with a chair," blurted from my mouth.

"Holy fuck Sherman, you're going mad," said Rob. He had a very serious look on his face. I turned to Ted and he also seemed to be in a state of concern.

What did they know that I didn't? Sure cocaine might make you a little hyper, but what had I done in my fit of laughter? I was sure that I wasn't getting the crazies. The crazies, or more aptly titled 'The Fits', is a condition that many people who venture towards the outskirts of their minds come into contact with. It's that point in your drug-induced state when you are so gone out of your mind that you have relinquished all control of your consciousness, to your sub-conscious mind. You begin to ride the wave and let it fling you off. It's quite disturbing to some people who know what 'The Fits' are when they encounter it; a person's sub-conscious can be a cavern of vile and demented things. It's nothing to be afraid of however. Getting to know your sub-conscious is an enlightening and fulfilling experience. The powers of the mind are infinite and when you create a loving relationship with your Self, life becomes even that more grand. It is simple. Once you have gone over the line, there is no coming back. Enjoy the experience and let your perception grow larger than you ever imagined.

"Yeah man, I think you've had enough. You just can't go around hitting girls with chairs man." Ted said roughly, as if I had just hit a woman with a chair. "You are way over the edge now man. I've never seen you like this before."

"Look, how about you motherfuckers stop your bitching and lets all have a beer and a line. That's no way to treat a future Doctor of Communication you know," I proclaimed. Who in the hell do they think they are? Fuck them and their motherly love. I'm going for the gold on this warm Monday night in August. Or is it morning? Oh well, it is of no importance. Thursday I will be in Las Vegas; Lord bless my soul. I wonder what the outcome is going to be of this spectacular weekend. See, my younger brother is getting married soon. Therefore, it is imperative that we go to Las Vegas for a weekend to indulge in all types of behavior unfit for a married man to be part of. If being in Las Vegas weren't enough, it is known to everyone involved that intentions are set for a singular energy of evil and destruction. This will be mine and my brothers seventh time venturing to Nevada's oasis of sin, but we have never had this level of chaos intended.

"Precious, beer please," I asked. "Just trying to prepare for Vegas."

"Brooooo," Rob elongated. "That shit is about to be stupid. Dog, I wish I was going. I know y'all are gonna have a ball."

"Hell yeah man. Niggas is gonna die."

"You stupid. Man, act a fool for me….," Rob paused and the mischievous grin slid across his face once again. "You should've invited shorty."

"Fuck you!"

For my anger, I received no gratification. I had invited 'shorty', Alexia. That's the name of my ex. She had recently broken up with me and moved to LA to pursue a career in porn. I'm sure you're wondering how in the hell I was too blind to see that coming. Hell, you've got to see that type of shit coming, right? Wrong. Long story short...her best friend moved to LA and pursued a career in porn, made $450,000 in a year, and quit. She moved to Houston, Texas and is currently pursuing a degree in chemical engineering in Houston. She also moonlights as a stripper...cold world. I should've saw that coming; Birds of a feather. These are now Alexia's ambitions, except she wishes to be a Lawyer. I called her four days ago and said that I would like for her to come to Vegas, and after a bit of prodding she agreed. We haven't seen one another in 5 months. As hell bent on destruction as I am, it's not going to hurt to have her along for the ride...plus if all else fails, I'll have sex in the palm of my hand. I'll play it off to the guys. Alexia has her own hotel at the Cosmopolitan anyway. All is good for a weekend of terror.

"Call a cab," I exclaimed. "I need to get my car. They might tow me."

THURSDAY, 8 A.M. EST

Where in the fuck is Corey? He was right behind us at the check-in line. Fuck it, the plane leaves in an hour and I certainly will not be late. I haven't been to sleep yet and I am anticipating the nap I am going to get on this four-hour plane ride, I thought to myself as my brother and I walked towards the screening and baggage check.

"You don't have anything on you do you?" I asked my brother. "I just had to toss a sack of weed into the trash can." My brother shook his head no and we continued on.

Ever since the September 11 attacks in 2001, Airports have undergone stupendous security upgrades. At Louisville International they have x-ray machines that passengers must stand in. Isn't this an invasion of privacy? A random person is able to see things that are invisible to the naked eye? What's worse is the fact that people cannot complain about this type of thing. At an International Airport in Houston, Texas, there have been reports of people not being able to complain about the groping and other excessive pat down tactics that TSA agents use on passengers when their x-ray scanners misidentify a metal button on a pair of pants as a weapon of mass destruction. In the instance of this debauchery, 'Not being able to complain' means that a voice over the loud-speaker explicitly states that you will be detained if you are heard making negative statements about the level of invasion to your person during their carry-on baggage screenings. I suppose that they are making strides in progression however. In Atlanta at another International Airport, due to a large number of arrests made for high-profile business travelers in possession of unchecked licensed handguns, a judge issued the decree that people will only be given citations instead of being arrested, in order to save money to the court system. This will also enable travelers to not miss their flights.

We made it through the screening without the TSA catching on to our scent of misery and loathing. While I put on my shoes, I looked back to see Corey making his way through the security screening. He made it through the x-ray scan, and then it happened. Murphy's Law came into full effect and no amount of positivity that I could muster was going to get us out of this pickle.

15

A TSA lady asked to see the palms of his hands. She brushed his hands with a powder and instantly motioned to several other agents. They shut down their lines and swarmed Corey like bee's to honey.

"Ayo, what the hell!" Corey cried, as four agents whisked him into an opaque glass room.

My brother and I stood astonished. It seemed like our trip to give hell all it bargained was going to end up as two brothers sulking over their friend being a terrorist. While we're in Vegas, he'll be getting shipped to Guantanamo Bay on charges of espionage. I knew the bastard was a secret agent. His Acapulco shirts and Italian loafer; he was too Johnny Depp in a society full of Justin Beibers...but he kept his act up for a long time. As we stood in a stupefied trance for what seemed like an eternity, I attempted to muster up a small bit of positivity, but it didn't seem to be working.

"Whatever happens, there is a reason. I don't know what in the fuck this is for but it's gotta end up nicely. The devil wants us to prosper."

I was trying to be as proactive about the situation as possible, but the look on my brother's face quickly brought what goodness I was feeling down to the size of a flea. Meditating had become one of my favorite activities and I find it imperative that I sit down and gather my Self by finding that space of peace, but god damn it this is my brother's last chance at being the greatest bachelor that the world has ever seen, and our cohort has been detained by pigs!

"It just had to be Corey. Flight leaves in 45 minutes and this is the shit that my bachelor's party has come too," My brother said. He was beyond annoyed and decided to take a seat. I joined him.

"Don't trip man, let's just breathe easy. I'm sure there's a great explanation for this nonsense. There's power in positive thought mane. Plus, Corey is a big boy...and he's white, so I'm sure they aren't handling him too rough". I tried to console my brother but he was very disturbed by the situation. The odd thing was that none of the other TSA agents paid us any attention. They let us sit on the outside of the security check point. Something good had to be brewing.

"I'm surprised they didn't take you in that little room. You could have a bomb stuck up your ass right now," I said to my brother in an attempt to lighten the mood.

"Fuck you. They probably won't let your bitch ass on the plane," He fired back with a smile. My joke seemed to be working.

A moment later, Corey waltzed out of the room with opaque glass walls with a large grin on his flush red face. My brother opened his mouth to speak but Corey shushed him and continued walking.

"Let's move swiftly, they think I'm Ronnie Depp."

My brother and I shook our heads and kept moving at a reasonable pace. We had to make a swift get away from these TSA queers and find the nearest bar, after we located our gate of course.

~

"What will you gentlemen be having today?" the waitress asked. She was a homely woman. I suppose that attractive bartenders didn't enjoy waiting tables at the airport much. It was pretty early in the morning though. Maybe the airport in Vegas would have better looking women.

"Drugs..." Corey uttered as he nonchalantly paged through an automotive magazine. "And Shelby is going to have some hooker pussy. How 'bout that lady? Can you handle that?"

Shelby, my brother whose name I hadn't given you all yet, could do nothing but shake his head and smile. You see, Corey and I are the epitome of ignorant. When immense idiocy meets supreme stupidity, demonic dunces such as Corey and I are born. Somewhere beneath the total mockery, the insignificance, the dishonesty, the innuendo, and the exaggeration between each sarcastic statement lies a significant truth...we truly give zero fucks. Add drugs, alcohol, and bad intention into the mixture and even Charles Manson would be squeamish. I don't think Shelby knew exactly what he was getting into with this excursion to Sin City.

"What in the hell Corey, that's no way to talk to this beautiful waitress of ours," I snapped back. The waitress' gaze at Corey was cold, as if she was calculating his murder.

"What? she asked what we'll be having TODAY...not right now. Sheesh. Go hit the pack man."

"What pack?" my brother interjected.

"Well guys, through all of that commotion back at security checkpoint, they neglected to find the one thing that got me put into that little room."

This sly fucking devil of a man had just done something remarkable. He had turned this monotonous plane ride into a Ferris wheel for the high life.

"He's an asshole so he needs toilet paper," my brother told the waitress. "And we'll all take Bourbon, straight up. Lot of liquor."

My brother's presence is a calming one. He is the only sane person out of the three of us. Let's see how long that lasts. As we sat and enjoyed our drinks, Corey told us of his encounter with TSA.

"Dude she rubbed my hands and looked at me funny. And then all of those motherfuckers surrounded me...I was for sure they were gonna make me strip. But I don't know if it was God or the devil, but the lady looked up at me and said 'I know you'. Corey's eyes became wide with excitement.

"That's when I knew I had her. The other three fucks were just looking at me so I said 'yeah well you probably know my brother. John. Yeah, I'm Ronnie. Ronnie Depp. I fly using an alias. It's not easy having an internationally famous sibling, you know?' The lady wanted a fucking hug and autograph," Corey said as he shook his head. "With that type of shit happening, this trip is gonna be fucking memorable."

About an hour into the flight, I dozed off for what seemed like an eternity, but was really only 30 minutes. In those 30 minutes, I came to the realization of a multitude of things. A dream that I had, which seemed much more like a vision than anything else, gave way to a new perspective. I was able to recall every detail of the dream, its lucidity allowing me to dictate everything happening, naturally. My pineal gland pumping dimethyltryptamine at an overdriven rate, when I awakened I felt that I had consorted with God, or the universe and its infinite power, or both...or maybe it was just a random dream. Sometimes that happens you know, especially when you didn't sleep the night before, and on Monday you decided to absolutely destroy any chance of having a productive week. We'll use God for this instance however... I felt that I had been with God. I believed the dream whole heartedly. One can become extremely enamored with his dreams and visions when he begins to pay attention to the lucidity of them. How quirky and radical they seem! Only a fool believes his dreams, and the fool is by far the greatest man. Harping about secrets told from ancient times with me, not knowing if it is the lack of sleep or my own inexplicable thinking making me have thoughts of a Grizzly Bear the size of a tool shed committing a gruesome murder. The poor dope had his head crushed and body slung in the air; the bear playfully jollying with the body of a man dressed in fly-fisherman garb. I sat addled on the porch of a house across the road. It was an old road, with sand colored dust and gravel. An open field sat to the opposite side of the road, which stretched for miles. Thickets of tall grass maintained residence along the road, while across from me a man that looked as if he should be on the cover of an outdoorsman magazine was being tossed around like a little girl would her doll whilst merrily skipping down a street. Oh, such joy this child must have. The guy wasn't bleeding though, so that was a good thing. Witnessing the folding of the mans' body by the bears' mouth as a seductive woman may do with her gum in attempts to woo one into a trance, I became upset and pointed a sniper rifle at the awful thing. "HOLY SHIT" wasn't the brightest thing to scream, especially after the damned creature sprouted wings out of the side of its spine. A humongous, disgusting, and vile a predator it was, with wings the length of telephone poles equipped with feathers. Of course the thing turned on me and discussing the situation with myself, I told myself that this episode wasn't going to end well. You know, not with a giant, feathered sadistic Grizzly Bear flying towards you. I kept wondering how this animal from crazy fantasy dream land was even able to fly; but that it did, and roaring towards me it was. Its mouth wide open, with saliva and mucus spewing from it as snot does from a sneezing toddler with a cold, I knew that I was fucked. And then it hit me. I realized what the bear and the man and the sniper rifle meant. As an egotistical and often drug induced individual, disturbing shit is not that "disturbing" to me. I am more disturbed by a person's choice between coffee and tea than I am by an active prostitute being your 15 year-old daughters' English teacher, so some things don't really bother me. We as human beings create our own perceptions, and some of us give a fuck while others don't. I happen to be one of those that don't. People often get it confused when one states "I don't give a fuck". It is often misinterpreted and misused. If you don't give a fuck, then you actually do. If you didn't give a fuck, it wouldn't be an issue. The bear represented a negative thought that I had been harboring regarding a female. Being in love with a person can easily turn to hate and hate is easily masked as love in the details of the actions associated with the words. Maintaining this negative thought, and by negative I mean one that is not conducive to receiving your desires, is a dismantling of the human spirit. It was tearing ass out of that poor sap of a man. Lord.

I woke to see Shelby becoming visibly frustrated due to a crying child and a drunken man making obnoxious comments and gestures. Corey seemed to be in a state of peace, and he should be, rightfully so. Between the Xanax and Bourbon, I'd say he was having a wonderful time. We're flying on a 747 jet, commercial passengers of course. Due to Corey's anxiety he was adamant that he sit nearest the walk way, and I despise anything but window seats, so Shelby was forced to sit in the middle. Poor Kid.

"Aye man where in the hell is the dope? Pass it here."

Whose voice was that? What in the hell? I opened my eyes to see my brother opening the gram of coke that Corey had snuck onto the plane.

"Bro, what in the hell are you doing?" I asked.

"Man, fuck yall. I gotta see what this shit is about."

I leaned forward and looked at Corey. He had that same grin he had on his face when he was walking away from the security checkpoint. I am surprised by my brothers' actions, but I won't dare stop him. Fuck that, turn up!

"Well shit, since you wanna be a grown up...dump the shit out."

"Right here? On the plane?"

"Hold on, hold on," Corey interjected. He raised his hands and shook them in unison with his head. "You don't take something like you're gonna do it and then question the professionals. Do as you're told, queer bait."

Shelby laughed deeply, looked around for would-be spies, and dumped the small bag of cocaine onto his tray table.

"This is the craziest thing I've ever done," Shelby whispered.

"Welcome to the club," I sarcastically replied.

"Man fuck the sentiments, let's get high," Corey said. Those Xanax must've been kicking into over drive.

Shelby reached into his pocket, pulled his driver's license from it and proceeded to break down the small rock into powder. While Shelby did that, Corey lowered his tray table and placed his carry-on bag on top of it.

"You know that's illegal right?" I mentioned as I nodded to Corey.

"And you know tooting powder on a commercial airline is illegal," Corey paused and looked at me. "And stupid as hell."

"Touché. But tooting powder isn't stupid!"

"Yeah, but that yell was. You're insane," Corey chided. He shook his head in disgust.

Fuck him. "Coming from the guy that told TSA he was Ronnie Depp, I'd say that was pretty normal. You ass."

"Fuck off," Corey laughed.

"Shut the fuck up and toot this powder kids. It's a long ass plane ride and a lot of cocaine sitting here." I looked at Shelby's tray table and saw 15 lines of blow. My eyes got large.

"I'm going to need a drink after this to calm my nerves. Shit. I can feel the adrenaline already," I said.

I pulled a $100 bill out of my pocket and rolled it into a straw. Shelby began doing the same, while Corey pulled a pre-rolled bill out of his pocket. My brother and I flashed Corey a look of disgust.

"What the fuck are ya'll looking at me like that for? Never seen a guy with a pre-rolled booger sugar bill?"

We shook our heads, and Shelby leaned down and sniffed his first line. Taking his index finger, he picked up the excess, rubbing it across his teeth.

"Who showed you?" I asked. It wasn't Yeezy."

"Nah," Shelby responded. "TV."

"Oh. Well, great teacher you had there."

Airplane rides to Las Vegas can be quite the circus. I wasn't expecting to have a quiet journey to Sin City, however I didn't expect the ride to be this ridiculous. Sure, here we are snorting lines of cocaine on a commercial airline, and one could call this activity incredibly stupid or incredibly genius, but this was no crasser than the middle aged white man wearing sunglasses, a floral print shirt, and khaki shorts chanting "nothing like Vegas" at the top of his lungs and guzzling shooters with no remorse. And our actions weren't anywhere near as creepy as the old geezer seated across the aisle from us, tonguing down his 23-year-old bimbo of a girlfriend. It's quite pitiful to see this type of act come in the form of a disgusting disparity, because you don't know who is using who and what for. Not to mention the voices of every fucking body on this damned plane, making the airwaves gyrate with despicable speech

21

of the tourist bullshit that they plan to participate in. Fuck them. I hope that they run into our crazed lunatic asses on Las Vegas Boulevard.

"Oh, you all are tourists?" I'd ask, holding a bottle of booze while wearing an over-sized sombrero and a costume Nazi mustache. "Well, today is your lucky day. See, we're tourists' too and we're here for just a little fun. Oh, what do we do for a living? Why are we here? Well, we're here to sacrifice small children and animals. May we borrow your son?"

Being so close to creepy and ignorant performance doesn't sit well with me due to the explicit fact that I am totally incapable of group behavior. If I see people doing something, I have to do the opposite.

"Too bad I'm all jacked up on Cocaine! Waitress, bring me some liquor!" I yelled to the front of the airplane.

"Asshole, press the fucking button," Corey blared back at me. "We're not even done with the candy, fucks your problem?"

And then she walked over; a gorgeous woman of 5'7-inch height with flowing blonde hair and not a hint cocaine residue in her nose.

"May I help you gentlem..." She tried to get the words out but they got caught in her throat. What is she thinking? Does she notice? Of course she notices. But does she care?

"May I ask what you gentlemen are doing back here?"

Oh no, it's too late! The flight attendant has caught on to our shenanigans. The best thing to do may be to take her hostage. I began looking around for anything that resembled a weapon.

"Well, we had ordered some powdered donuts and we wanted to know if you wanted any," Shelby said, trying to make light of the situation. It's not every day that a stewardess would see a tray table full of cocaine being lackadaisically used by two black guys and Ronnie Depp.

"No, I'm on a diet. You do know that I could get you all into major trouble right? It's 9 a.m. for crying out loud."

"Oh, that late? But, yeah we do and see, that's why we need your help. We're small town boys on our way to Las Vegas in order to chase the American Dream and seeing that all we've learned from is television and movies, we thought this would be appropriate. You see, this man right here," Shelby nudged my shoulder, "Is a future Doctor of Communication that must write a dissertation about the illegal slave trade that is prostitution and why it is so wildly popular."

"The American Dream, huh? Sounds like you're searching for Hell in Vegas. That's easy. Try searching for Heaven," the flight attendant replied, giving us a skeptical look in the process.

"But of course," Corey chimed in as he squinted at her name tag, "Melody."

"Well, look here boys. Getting that shit on a plane is a commendable feat, so fuck it. I'm not going to ask any questions but you motherfuckers owe me a tip and some of that shit. I'll be back with some alcohol and my phone number. I'll be stuck in Vegas for 2 days. I'm with you all." Melody turned around and walked off.

"What the fuck just happened?" I asked. "We just made a fucking friend for Vegas? Fuck yeah! Now if we get low on money we can pimp her out! As candid as she is, I'm sure she'd be down to make us a couple thousand extra bucks. The broad talks like a fucking sailor!"

"Why you always gotta think that women are hoes and will be down for that type shit?" Shelby questioned me as if he didn't already know what my answer would be.

"My ex, prick..." I said without paying him much attention.

"Dude you've been fondling her for an hour, just suck her titties, why don't you? Give us a little peep too." Corey was visibly upset when I looked at his face after raising my nose from the tray table.

"Do y'all see this bullshit? Old fucking man playing with titties and doesn't want to give the other passengers a peep show. This is a shame! Show us her fucking titties or fuck off!"

And then it happened. The woman hopped up and took off her blouse and slid her panties down, flinging both garments at Corey, unzipped the old man's pants and sat down. Wow. This trip to Vegas is definitely being controlled by Satan.

"There we go! That's what I'm talking about!"

Melody came back with our drinks, and upon seeing the sexual act going on across from us and hearing Corey cheering them on, grabbed a bill sitting on the tray table, leaned over, and snorted two long lines of cocaine.

"You motherfuckers are some funny ass people. This is going to be a good weekend."

It's 9 A.M. on a Thursday and I've seen drugs, liquor and sex. None of which belong to me. Such is life in Las Vegas, or Heaven.

THURSDAY, 9:30 A.M PST

"Hey Pedro, what's going on? Yeah, we just landed. Where are we headed? To the hotel once we grab our bags. Ok great."

Walking through the airport with glazed eyes the size of dinner plates wasn't what I intended for this day, however, it was a pleasant surprise. With the plane ride over and our lives sure to take sudden twists and turns due to our drug induced reasoning, it is easy to allow your imagination the opportunity to run wild and let the uncertainty and mystery of today make your life great. Plus, we had to make it to our bags, and that task in itself is something worth telling.

~

Shelby berated a couple of gray haired geezers who were upset that he stood idle on the walking side of the travellator, while Corey knocked over trash cans and barely dodged the rage of a crew of neurotic TSA agents in a golf-cart while walking backwards, after we stepped off of the moving walk-way. In his mind, walking backwards was a bright idea that would make him see the world clearer. Between their insolence and thoughtless unawareness, and my wandering spirit, it took us 30 minutes to locate baggage claim. Throughout our search, I realized that this weekend had no choice but to be a grand experience of inacceptable entertainment.

"Dude my fucking bag...Where the fuck is it?" said Corey. His face was intense and I wondered what he so desired his bag for. We had just gotten to the baggage claim.

"Patience my son," I retorted, "They'll be here shortly."

"Fuck a shortly damn it. I need the bag!" Corey said before mumbling under his breath, "I got more drugs."

I eyed Corey with a stare of disbelief. What should I have expected from him? To not be fully-equipped for a weekend rendezvous with enough drugs to disable a bull Elephant? That's inconsistent with who Corey was as a person; always prepared and always willing to get you totally fucked up.

The bags whirled around the baggage claim and we each picked up our own and headed towards the exit, slowly, as to not draw any attention to the fact that Corey had also picked up another person's luggage. Great. Theft in an airport and we JUST LANDED!

Once we stepped outside into the prickly dry heat of the desert in August, hell manifested. As Corey waved down a cab, a loud yell came from baggage claim.

"You fucking nigger give me my bag!" a middle aged white man screamed.

The three of us looked at each other in bewilderment and proceeded to race towards the cab, Shelby holding luggage in both hands. It is amazing how fast and strong a person becomes when he has the effects of cocaine coursing through his body. It is also amazing how stupid people can be. Why are we running anyway? Are we trying to bring attention to ourselves? Reaching the taxi first due to my past as an all-state member of the high school track team, I tapped the window and told the driver to open the trunk. The cab driver hesitated, so I placed my face to the driver's side window and said forcefully, "Open the fucking trunk." Luckily the bastard complied.

Shelby and Corey rushed past and threw their luggage into the trunk, and I did the same. I thought to myself why the guy didn't chase us? Why weren't we stopped? They both hopped into the back seat and ducked as low as possible.

"What in the fuck…" I whispered before turning to the cab driver. "Bally's, please and thank you."

I reached into my pocket and pulled out a rolled up hundred-dollar bill from my pocket and handing it to him.

"Go easy on the incense and hummus next time man," Shelby said from the backseat. The cab driver's eyes creased as he stared at Shelby through the rearview mirror.

"Is it safe to drive with them, is everything alright? I do not condone criminal activity in my cab," the driver asked sarcastically. His accent made him seem extremely cartoonish to a coked out motherfucker like myself.

"Come on Abu, shut up and drive," I heard Shelby chirp from the back seat, while Corey handed the man another $100 bill.

"Is that good for you?" Corey asked, waving the cash in the drivers face. "Come on man. that's $200 bucks. Get us to the fucking Nipple."

The cab driver hesitated, then grabbed the money and quickly stuffed it into his pocket, threw the gear in drive and screeched away from the airport.

Once away from airport property, I turned around and cursed the two dipshits in the backseat.

"What in the fuck dude? Drugs and you two motherfuckers do not mix! Just wait 'til we get to the room." Damn it to hell. Who did I think I was? I sound like an alcoholic father telling his son not to drink liquor. But, I was seriously disturbed by what had just transpired. Two heathens lay in the back seat giggling while my heart raced at 100 miles an hour. What in the fuck kind of beginning to the American Dream was this? Maybe I wasn't really in search of the American Dream. Maybe I was just searching for a place to get my twisted and demented rocks off. What had the flight attendant meant by Heaven in Las Vegas? Las Vegas could be considered Heaven in some respects I suppose; all of a persons' wildest fantasies and desires coming to life. There isn't a shortage of anything in that sinful desert of a utopia, where the angels come to frolic with mortals and the demons teach the humans how to destroy. Could Heaven really be in Las Vegas? I was going to find out.

As we cruised down Swenson St, the window down and dry desert air beating my face, I eyed the local University through my aviator style sunglasses. A left on East Harmon and a hidden right by Planet Hollywood brought us to a screeching halt and the relatively empty side entrance to Bally's.

"Glad I got that early check-in," I said aloud, to no one in particular. The cab driver looked at me out of the side of his eye, but that's about the only reaction that I received. See, I despise evening and night departure flights and I'll be damned if I arrive in a city after 4 P.M. Fuck that. It doesn't matter what bells and whistles or stupid ass policy rules I have to make those receptionists forget, I always get it done. I made sure that the rooms were ready last night. People will do a lot of things for you if you tell them that you need the rooms to shoot a few social media models.

"Hello, yes my name is Lars Randolph, photographer for Interweb Babes. I booked two rooms under pseudo names recently, Sherman Smith and Corey Curran…yes I'll hold please…two suites? Yes, yes that is us. Well, I booked the suites for the weekend and the girls and I and our other photographer are getting into town early in the morning, is there any way that we could get an early check in? Yes, I'll hold again…It's no problem? Ya sure? Ok great, wonderful. We'll be arriving around 10 A.M… Thanks."

There's something about the afternoon and evening that makes me feel like I missed my entire day. The morning is a wonderful time of the day; it gives you a chance to claim and exclaim that greatness and goodness will unfold for the next 24 hours. Looking out of the car window, I wasn't able to spot one bell hop. This could be a good thing or bad thing but it's probably better for the lot entrance to be empty than packed, with these two wag's hell bent on witlessness. The only other people present was a throng of Chinese people unloading from a giant white tour bus near the doorway. Great, now I have to combat a school of over excited tourists that love to snap cameras and mistake random people for famous musicians and actresses.

"Oh shit look, The Flamingo is across the street. That'll do wonders for my meditations." Corey said while hopping out of the vehicle.

I stepped out of the car puzzled.

"The Flamingo? What the fuck does that have to do with anything?"

I'm extremely confused as to what is going through this man's head. But whatever. Bad decisions make good stories.

"I've always wanted to trash a Flamingo hotel room so I figure I may as well manifest it. The visual was good for it."

I raised my eyebrows and nodded my head back. What in the hell has gotten into this guy? Yes, Zen is helpful to a lot of things and I find it a great practice to find that inner peace, but what in the hell is this guy up to?

"Pedro!"

What in the hell was Shelby yelling at? I looked up to see a six feet three, two hundred and eighty-pound colossus of a man approaching us, carrying nothing but a plastic grocery bag. If I didn't recognize him I'd feel a bit threatened because the guy looks menacing as hell. There are ugly people in the world but this man is truly ugly.

"Hey buddy," the cab driver muttered as he lifted the trunk. I turned to see him tossing our bags to the ground with no regard. What if I was carrying an urn?

"I am leaving!"

I could barely get a word out before he had all of our shit on the ground and was back inside his car. I gave him the middle finger as he screeched off. I hope he saw it.

"What's wrong with that guy?" Pedro chirped, his voice sounded as if he'd inhaled a dozen helium balloons. When we were kids, he had a high-pitched voice, but I would have assumed that he grew out of it during those 6 years in the pen.

Suddenly, Corey burst into laughter and Pedro gave him a look that would shake even the angel Michael to his knees. Still, Corey did not pause.

"What the fuck you laughing at sunshine?" Pedro flared, visibly upset.

Corey continued laughing. Pedro was ready to punch him out when Corey raised his arm and screamed "He has on a tutu!"

After hearing that, Pedro lowered his hand and his face lightened. I was surprised by the action but didn't want to ruin the moment, so I hushed my mouth and shook Pedro's hand.

"He's on acid?" Pedro asked.

"Acid? What in the flying fuck do you mean acid? Like LSD? Is that what we took?! Fuck you Corey!" Shelby screamed in a fit of rage before he was hit him like a mac truck. "Aww man, fuck. Fuck. Fuck. Fuck. Why in the fuck is a dancing alligator coming towards us?!"

"Little cuz, calm down," Pedro said. He grabbed Shelby's head and stared into his eyes. "Calm down alright? You're just hallucinating. That's it. Enjoy it man. Enjoy it."

"Dude, get the fuck off of me your hair is on fire!" Shelby roared. He ripped his head out of Pedro's grip and turned to Corey, who was still laughing his ass off.

"I mean I understand that I'm tripping but shit, a goddamn warning would've been nice!"

"Well look, guys, here's your bag. I made it real good." He paused and then turned around. "You all enjoy your fucking day." Pedro dropped the bag on the ground and began walking towards the direction that he came from. I yelled after him. m

"How much!?"

He casually threw a hand in the air, "I got drugs to sell. These fiends can't serve themselves, you know."

Pedro was an odd kid growing up. He was always the biggest

kid, but he never got picked first. Not to block in backyard football, not to read in class, not even to see his mother's funeral. He had to choose between standing on the wall of the church sanctuary and being seated in the back of the church on the last pew. He was a beast of a man however. He was sent to prison when he was 20 for punching a customer in the forehead at his grandfather's restaurant. The guy died on the spot. Pedro ended up pleading guilty to a manslaughter charge after it was found that the customer berated Pedro for not filling his cup of water swiftly enough. Pedro often said that he'd do it all over again if he had to.

"Pedro the dancing bear, holy shit!" Corey was still at it. I turned around to see him lying on the pavement with his feet propped on his luggage. Shelby sat on a bench near the entrance to the hotel, holding his head between his legs and rocking back and forth. Acid? Corey was whispering about Acid? Holy fucking shit. What in all high hell was going on? Sure, a little MDMA, cocaine and pot never hurt anyone...but acid? I'd never tried the shit and from the looks of it Shelby hadn't either. I reached down and picked up the plastic shopping bag that was near my feet, looked around, and opened it. Rummaging through it, I found that inside was a package of a dozen red paper cups and paper plates, a screw driver, a packet of picture wall-mounts, petroleum jelly, and a folded manila envelope. Where were the drugs? What in the hell Pedro? I decided that we had better go and check into the hotel so I could look through the bag. Maybe he had hidden things somewhere.

"Hey kids, it's time to go and check in. Corey, you got yourself right? Come on."

Corey, still lying on the ground, casually lifted a bucket hat that covered his face and began rising. His lime green Acapulco shirt, with flying toucans and parrots strewn across it in no particular order or pattern, was covered with sweat and asphalt. He looked like he stank.

"Yeah right behind ya."

"Shelby, I'm going to check in. chill right here," I said. I hope he doesn't move.

~

Walking into a casino in Las Vegas is like no other experience on earth. Its surreal...the lights and visions and funny looking foreign bartenders and table hands. Upon entering, you become instantly energized; dopamine and serotonin rushing through your brain, your adrenaline pumping in over-drive. Your heart races like a jack rabbit on crack in an orgy with 10 other jack-rabbit chicks. You want to conquer the world and the world you will conquer. Until you're flat broke wishing to go home because Vegas has gotten the best of you. Las Vegas is not designed for the average person to get the most out of. Sure, you can lounge around in the comfort of your hotel, walk through malls connected to more hotels, go to the great pool with the dope ass pool party that happens to be at your hotel, and even get drunk at the best clubs that happen to be at your hotel. Walk The Strip in sweltering heat until your sandals melt into the pavement and the sun block lotion that you pasted onto your body is dripping from you, if you'd like. Fuck it. You're sure to find lots of fun and create great memories, some of which you won't remember because you're too shitfaced and have fallen into the bushes. Yes, you'll master the art of standing on couches if you live the life of Las Vegas like a drunken tourist. After all, the only reason you go to Vegas is for the party. But this is not the life for those who really want to get the most out of Las Vegas, and all of the quirkiness and ridiculousness that resides there. In order to see Las Vegas stark naked in all of her glory, you've got to give in to the dark side. You've got to let the bitch that is Las Vegas take you for the ride. As has been for millennia, the only reason human beings agonize is due to their inherent need to take seriously what the gods of the earth, the presenters of secret & imagination or whatever the fuck you want to call it, made for pleasure. Everything in Las Vegas was made for pleasure; delve into all that is pleasurable and all that is right in Las Vegas. Go for the ride. You can be nice to Las Vegas all you want but she will not be nice back, under any circumstance…if you do it the right way. Explore. Destroy. Corrupt. Disgust. And most of all, remain happy.

I proceeded into the lobby and my whole world changed. Bells, whistles, gadgets, cards, and enough alcohol to drown Ohio…this is what I came here for…this must be God-ordained. Hell, I get to witness Corey ballroom dancing with an invisible girlfriend. I say invisible because after I asked him:

"What in the flying fuck are you doing?", to which he responded,

"Dancing with Bella, my invisible girlfriend."

This guy is ridiculous. And this acid stuff, man...he seemed to be having a lot of fun, but Shelby wasn't quite all there. Due to the law of averages, I deduced that I would be in the middle of their extremes, so I made a mental note to inquire to Corey in total secrecy under penalty of espionage and treason in regards to a blotter. The line was relatively short and I approached the counter, making sure that Corey was still close behind. He was busy standing at a nearby wall, whispering in an imaginary ear with his arm wrapped around the shoulder of his imaginary girlfriend.

In five minutes I was back to Corey with my room keys.

"Go get your keys man. I'll wait here by your luggage."

Corey didn't bother speaking and strolled off towards the reservation counter, arm still wrapped around the imaginary girlfriend named Bella. Bella had better be pretty.

Five minutes...ten minutes....15 minutes passed before Corey came back over.

"Hey, hairs on fire," Corey said with a chuckle.

"What took you so long man? Hopefully Shelby didn't run off," I said as we began to leave.

"Sorry. She wanted to argue with me about my girlfriend. She said she couldn't give me towels for two on account of me not being able to prove I had a girlfriend. She was standing right next to me though! I mean I tongued her down and was gonna fuck her to prove it if I had too, but the lady eventually complied. Only thing is, my girl ran off with a big old Caveman looking motherfucker riding a goddam Wolly Mammoth. His Acapulco shirt was nice though."

I looked at Corey, puzzled, and continued walking. As I stepped outside, I noticed Shelby standing on a bench, casting an imaginary fishing rod.

"Look at this fuck. I didn't give him much. He's good now." Corey said as we walked towards the wanna be fly-fisherman.

"Hey guy, watch out for the water and don't be too loud. You'll scare the fish away."

Corey and I looked at each other and instinctively had the same idea. We began walking in front of Shelby until he eventually freaked.

"Alright white and black Jesus, walking on water. Cool trick, but you're scaring my fish away!"

All of a sudden, Corey jumped into the air and I followed suit, stomping down on the puddle of asphalt. Up, down, up, down, we jumped. Fuck it, why not drive this loon crazy. I'm sure he is going to get his revenge once I begin hallucinations of the rapture and little green goblins climbing out of the wall.

"For crying out loud you fuck's scared all of the fish away! Fuck!"

"Shut up, let's go to the room," I exclaimed, still jumping. Shelby hopped down from the bench, picked up his bag and the other bag and walked into the hotel. Corey and I followed.

"Can Las Vegas be Heaven?" I asked while walking towards the elevators. The casino inside of Bally's was lit brightly, with people everywhere. While we walked towards the casino elevators, I noticed pint sized bottles of gin inside of the gift shop. To my right was the casino pit, which stretched the entire lobby. Craps, blackjack, poker, & roulette dealers shuffled cards and spun their machines. Slot machines went off all around us, the click of the slot arms coming down, machines sounding off as they rotated. An occasional shout from a patron erupted through the many voices of people on the first floor of the hotel where the casino was. The uproar was usually followed by curse words.

"I don't see why not," Corey responded, turning towards the gift shop. "Might as well get some liquor man."

I suppose Las Vegas could be Heaven, seeing that in all actuality Heaven is wherever you want it to be. Heaven is supposed to be all good, right? All good feelings, all good thoughts. I mean, who doesn't like thinking about cool and good shit? And who doesn't like feeling good? Sure, you may have used a couple of mind altering stimulants to make yourself feel that good, and sure you may have once had misogynistic thoughts of an orgy with 4 Blonde Russians, unbothered by the fact that you're on a "business trip" with the company banking cards, while your two children and wife are at home. You're feeling good, loving your life and everything in it. But you also know that when you get back home, you will be back in hell; with a griping wife and two terribly obnoxious children at home, you work 16 hour days in order to stay as far away from them as long as you possibly can. The company that you and your best friend run is doing wonderful, but every other part of your life is terrible. Your wife won't have sex with you and your kids are the worst brats since the little bastard boy from hell. But in Las Vegas, you have women at your fingertips, the finest gourmet meals, the best of the best in narcotics, all of which make you FEEL good. You want to continue this 'feel good' but you know that it is only temporary, because soon you will return to hell. In foreseeing the future that lies ahead, you resolve to do as much as you possibly can. When you get home, you are still on such a high that nothing can stop you, even though you are in utter misery. But hell, things aren't so bad. The kids are a little more tolerable, the wife is nagging less. You're a happier you because you just enjoyed one hell of a weekend...one that you can keep in secrecy or tell to a close buddy over a cold beer. You'll proclaim that life is quite alright. That's the beauty of Las Vegas...it can be Heaven and make you feel good in the future, even in hell. But if you do it right...if you do it the way that it was designed, you will be thankful to be alive. You will be thankful that you made it back to where you came from and are out of Las Vegas. Yes, in your head you will be mounting your return to the bitch, but you dare not utter the words until you are back squarely where you came from. Las Vegas should provide such a spiritual awakening that this Mecca of Sin becomes a refuge for you to purify. Las Vegas should kill you. Not in the literal sense. Las Vegas has all of your hearts desires, just like Heaven.

Inside of the gift shop I rummaged around, picking things up and placing them in the wrong place. Shelby stood in one spot, fascinated by a rack of key chains while Corey was busy grabbing two pints of orange juice out of a sliding cooler.

"Can I get two bottles of gin?" Corey asked.

The cashier walked towards the wall and grabbed two of the pints. Corey looked at her with wild eyes.

"Hey lady I want fifths. Do you have fifths? I see fifths of everything else and you grab pints."

"No," the cashier said sternly, before walking back to the register and ringing up the bottles.

"$52."

"$52 for two pints of gin and some OJ? Damn you mother fuckers are getting over," Corey said as he reached into his back pocket. He pulled out his debit card, handed it to the cashier, and grinned. "Let me get your discount."

The cashier, a homely Latina, didn't respond. She finished ringing Corey up and handed him his card without uttering a word.

"Honestly, it's not that hard to be a good fucking person,"

Corey said angrily.

I giggled, wondering what he is seeing. That acid shit is crazy. How am I going to react to it? Will I even react at all? Who knows...What will I see? Hopefully it wouldn't be anything demonic, because that would suck. Devils, goblins and ghouls riding into the casino through the ceiling on billowing brimstone, some even taking time to stop by the performance stage which sits across from the bar, and do a small dancing number while an impersonator serenades the crowd of blue and orange giraffes and pink jungle monkeys. That would be seriously insane to say the very least and I'm not quite sure how I would react to that scenario. Would I bug out? Would I be afraid? Or would I laugh and enjoy the zoo that I see before me. One thing is for sure, I am willing to find out.

"Corey, meet us at our room in about an hour. 2675," I said to Corey as the three of us stepped off of the elevator, immediately being introduced to the mirrors that line the hallway. Shelby and Corey instantly looked to the ground and for a second I wondered if I should too.

"Alright, cool. I'm in 2673 anyway," Corey responded, assuring me that he was he alright.

They gave us rooms near each other which was convenient because telling Corey to meet us in an hour means he'll meet us in three. He's worse than black people when it comes to being on time. The bastard is going to be late to his own funeral, too busy combing his hair to notice that he's been dead a week.

I wonder aloud if the rooms are connected.... I can't distinguish between if that scenario would be a good thing or a bad thing. It could quit possibly be both. Fuck it; I won't force anything. I'll just allow. Ride the wave? Right... It's like the Great Master discoursed...be like water. Not pulling, not pushing; only going with the flow of everything. Something may pull, you go with it. Something pushes, you give. I'll everything and be unstoppable. Let action take its course. Eventually all of the pieces fall into place, so lark at the perplexing nature of life and virtuously exist in the now. Shit happens and most often times for a reason. One of the greatest parts of it all is that moments are temporary. Find joy in the now and in being present at all times because moments never last forever. And now that I don't give a fuck what happens, I've got to be present in the now and get my brother to the room so he doesn't look at any of the perpetual mirrors in this hallway and see his face melting. Who in the fuck would put mirrors on every wall surface on this floor? This is ridiculous.

We marched down the hall and I couldn't help but notice that Corey wasn't looking down anymore. He instinctively noticed my confusion and offered up a quick explanation.

"I'd rather look at myself as a rotting corpse than to have to pay attention to the tightrope I'm walking on. There's a lava pit down there. You're floating on a cloud, skinny Buddha. Shelby's gonna die."

"Fuck you," said Shelby, as he closed his eyes into a tight clinch.

Under much duress, we eventually made it to our rooms. Shelby and I bid Corey adieu as he handed me a bottle of alcohol and a bottle of juice. Once I opened the door, I noticed that the rooms weren't connected. They were right next door to each other however, so that was pretty cool. I tossed my bags on the floor and Shelby followed suit. We had deluxe suites for the weekend, so if we ended up tearing shit up, boy oh boy would it cost somebody. I say somebody because after all, I do know of a porn star staying at The Bellagio. The sofa bed may really come in handy.

The walls in the room were covered in drab beige paint and pictures of landscapes that looked like a six year-old using water color paints drew them. Shelby and I lay down on our separate beds and I imagined the ridiculousness that was in store for this weekend. With my level of intoxication about to be at an all-time high, I fully expected to be the reason that the second coming commenced; Jesus would float down from the beam of Excelcior. Either way, I wondered what I could manifest. Believe, trust and detach. Or maybe not, it is my brother's bachelor's weekend after all. It's all up to him; I'll bask in the uncertainty of every single moment afforded to me. I am the captain of my own mind and I'm not too cool with being a victim of my own thinking. That's mightily counter-productive. It's ok to be intimate with my personal darkness, but to let it destroy me and my way of thinking would mean that it is under control. NOPE. I wonder if I should call the flight attendant. And what in the hell am I going to do about Alexia? Nobody knows that she's even here. I'm sure she'll call me sometime today or tomorrow, no worries. I didn't bother asking when she would be in town, only gave her dates that I'd be here. With that dream I had earlier though, I'd be happy if she didn't call.

THURSDAY, 9 P.M. PST

"What if tattoos randomly popped up on our skin at certain points in our lives, like key points in our lives? And we had to figure out what the newest tattoo meant through a subjective observation of ourselves…like, we had to figure out what they meant for us so that we could move on to the next stage in our lives?" I asked to no one in particular. I do this often when I am full of contemplation, hoping that someone will lend me an idea as to ascertain if what I know is something worth expressing to others. The four of us were walking down Las Vegas Boulevard, headed towards The Bellagio to gamble on the electronic machines at the bar. Place twenty bucks in the machine, get comp'd all night for liquor whilst playing. Entertain the bartender and tip him every now and then, you'll be drinking free the whole weekend.

"Well, I mean, would everyone have the same tattoos with the same meanings at different periods in their lives or would they have the same tattoos with different meanings for each person?" Melody asked. I looked at her in surprise; she's interested in things like this? I'm high off of my ass on a hit of acid, and looking at her brought nothing more than a shimmer of light in the form of a face and a head full of bright yellow daisies.

"I suppose it would have to do with a person's emotions," I said as we stepped ahead in front of Corey and Shelby. Their acid highs have ended and the cocaine that is flowing through their bodies has taken control. Oh, sorry. Excuse my rudeness, Melody is the flight attendant. "Does logic supersede emotion or does emotion supersede logic? Most people are emotionally driven and are easily manipulated due to their emotional response…"

"Yes and," Melody butted in. I squinted my eyes and gazed at her. "All logic is limited by ones' knowledge. If you're ignorant on any one subject, then your logic regarding that subject is flawed."

"Right… And most people don't know shit!" I exclaimed as we erupted into laughter. "It's kind of like, if I don't know much about you as a person, then my logic regarding you is terrible. I make assumptions and use guttural response."

"Oh, so you're one of those feeling type guys," Melody

nudged my ribs and flashed a glowing face smile. Her daisies shined brighter.

"Nah, I'd call it instinct," I laughed back, "and my gut instinct is telling me that you're a jokester. You're pretty though."

It was refreshing to have an intelligent conversation with someone of the opposite sex. Often times, especially whilst in party capitals of the USA, such as Las Vegas or Miami, it is all about sex and money. Fun times, but it does nothing for the re-wiring of the brain, the next evolutionary step of man. We've gotten rid of unnecessary organs and attributes as far as the human species is concerned and in my opinion, the only thing left to do is re-open our blind eye. Increase our own capacity for happiness and operate on the frequency of happiness, love, and desire.

The Las Vegas Strip is a beautiful sight, with the beautiful lights of the casinos and hotels, the bustle of people going to and from. The weather is perfect and the air is wonderfully electric, you can sense the excitement in it. Tonight is Thursday and we promised ourselves that we would take it easy and destroy our bodies Friday and Saturday nights. Melody is leaving Saturday morning, so that gave Corey, Shelby, and I one night to wreak havoc on everything that moved in Las Vegas. I'm not too sure how well we are going to uphold our promise, seeing that Pedro left us a quarter of the best cocaine that I have ever seen, an eighth of an ounce of MDMA, and a sheet of 20 acid hits on blotter paper. We had brought enough cocaine to last throughout the night, and Melody wanted to bring MDMA, so of course we allowed it. She said that it was her favorite drug and that one day she had stayed up for 10 days on a binge. She also said that she was able to complete 45 flights in those ten-days. I'm not sure how flight attending works, but good Lord. Good fucking Lord.

Sidenote: I'm sure you all are wondering how Melody even got with us. And that in itself is an epic saga of a lifetime wrapped up in a 10-hour debacle of time, but I'll keep it short.

We got into our rooms around 10:30 A.M. Shelby and I rested until Corey decided to knock on the door around noon. Shelby kept speaking of his fascination with the neon green and purple lizards crawling on the walls, so I'm not sure how much rest he got. As soon as Corey came in, we cracked the bottle of Bombay and the orange juice and poured ourselves drinks. While we drank, I decided to open the supply bag that Pedro had dropped off, and dumped the items out. The contents floated across the mahogany tinted desk that Corey and I sat at. Shelby sat in a large chair, staring out of the hotel window. The view wasn't spectacular, but it wasn't horrible either. A parking garage sat in the foreground, and in the background were numerous hotels. In the distance you could see the 'New York New York' Hotel sign. I bet it looks nice in the night time hours. Las Vegas itself is a bright star in a black pit. It shines bright like a fire in the darkness of the desert. The city of sin, lit up like Lucifer.

"What in the fuck is the screw driver for?" Corey asked as he picked it up. He then lifted the cups and turned them upside down and out fell a boulder of cocaine with a loud thud, so loud that it made Shelby turn around. "I'm not doing that shit. It's turning different shades of blue, and glowing. That can't be good."

In reality, it looked like the bottom half of a snowman that a kid would make in their front yard. Corey and I looked at one another with lit up faces. I grabbed and examined it, in awe of the way it shimmered and shone, like the scales on an aquatic gilled animal.

"All rock G," I said as I set the rock the size of Montana back on the table. I grabbed the paper plates, tore the plastic packaging, selected one, and placed the blow on it. Grabbing the screwdriver, I held it by its head and tapped the rock once, breaking it into few pieces. I smacked each large piece into smaller and more portable pieces and placed them all back into the bag except for two dime sized rocks.

"This shit must've just come off of the brick. Pedro! We love you!"

Corey, Shelby, and I laughed heartily and as we drank and tooted powder with reckless abandon at 12:15 on a Thursday afternoon, we engaged in conversation about everything from life to religion. There is something about the properties of cocaine that will turn you into a motor mouthed chatter box, bringing new and refreshing thoughts into your mind and out of your mouth. Most intoxicants do this however.

Long ago, I stopped following ideas that others had of what my life should be. Most people have never stepped out of their own paper bag of a life to understand other people or different types of shit in the world, simply relying on their own logic and perception to guide them. Those twisted fucks. They are the ones who disagree with the way we live, the ones who try to impose their way of living onto us so that we can validate it. Fuck you and your life. I do not feel the need to allow you to validate my life so why on earth do you feel the need for me to validate yours? Are you living right? Am I living wrong? Small people who are caught up in petty and individual personal causes, getting in the way of serious change are like this. You sit and judge others and wonder why people judge you. You do not have gratitude for what you have and continue the downward spiral of living in mental, social, and economic poverty. 98% of the inhabitants of this world are in the same boat; systemically impoverished, and majority do not know it.

The looming issue here is that mounds of individuals believe that economic deficiency is the worst type of systemically implemented poverty there is, yet mental and social poverty have enabled individuals to create these issues for others. This cycle is never ending, because of the 98%...Because of your, our complaints, we are not awarded anything in abundance. We are joyful and blissful and full of fun and I say we, not as in Corey, Shelby and I, but we as in the people of this world who are open-minded enough to bask in the uncertainty of everything. We're called the 'weirdo's' because we realize that God moves in our thoughts. We relax and accept our good, which is all that is coming to us. The belief that things happen, and how we choose to perceive these things, in terms of good or bad, dictate the experience that it will give us. Operating on a high level of happiness, which takes time, is the key to fulfilling this universal language. I bask in the stillness of life and the perfectness of now. Those people who make attempts to box you in and understand something of you that is not in the positive light shall forever drown in their own misery of unfulfilled desire. I am the mirror to your ignorance. If any one thing was ever postulated in regards to my person by another, it was twisted from and fashioned by their own character. Be you, do you; live you. In meditation and the search inside of myself, I have come to know that truth is inside of my soul, all I needed to do was listen in silence to find out the answer to every question that I have ever had.

"You ready for the married life bro?" I asked as I took another toot of powder from the paper plate and passed it to Shelby. He snorted a line and passed the plate to Corey, looked at me and shook his head.

"Yeah man, I'm ready. Shit, it's like we're married anyway. Girls just want rings and fly shit to make it official."

I've never understood marriage in the sense of paper work and rings and ceremonies, it's a bit of over-kill if you ask me. It's a spiritual process, in my opinion, so all of the hoopla and bullshit is not needed. Adam and Eve were married but did they have a damned wedding? I'm not too sure.

"Yeah," I reply, "You'll be a pretty decent husband. Just don't cheat on her."

"Yeah man, be cool how you be cool. You've been faithful the whole relationship though, right?" Corey chimed as he passed the plate back over to me.

"Most definitely, it isn't that hard to have self-control. Plus, she is gorgeous so I'm fine with what I've been fucking. The key is to not have your woman cheat on you."

"And how do you go about that, relationship guru?" I questioned, as the cocaine flowing up my nostrils burned my sinus cavity. "This shit is so damn strong. Damn!"

"Man I swear I'm going to have a relationship talk show, I can fix any niggas issues with his woman. Here's the key man," Shelby adjusted himself in his chair and slowly poured himself another drink as Corey and I looked at him intently. "Deep down my niggas, bitches don't desire a volume of men. Sure, you have your cases of bitches that just like to fuck people, and we call them prostitutes and porn stars. Women though, the ones good enough to marry, simply desire a volume of emotions. It doesn't matter how they come."

"Is that why you see pretty girls with ugly ass men?" I asked, turning my cup to my face to finish the last of my drink. "Hell yeah…warm Bombay and OJ, why didn't we get any ice?"

Shelby shook his head and continued his display of wit while I poured another drink. Corey was stuck, sitting in his chair and staring out of the window. I wondered what in the hell he was thinking about, he must be seeing some awfully crazy shit.

"Niggas though, we like combinations and packages. As long as she can change her look, we're amused. We can feel the same shit over and over without it becoming boring and shit, if we have something new to look at. The girl cuts her hair or something, a wardrobe change, it could be anything."

"Oh, aren't you such a smart man," Corey piped, surprising Shelby and I. "But, ladies like that too. Where's the flight attendants number? I'd like to call her."

~

Day or night, you can see anything on the Las Vegas Strip. Men in diapers, bums, people trying to pass you escort cards. There's such a variety of stupid shit that will utterly amaze you on The Strip that I'll be damned if I ever go to one of those cockamamie acrobat or magic shows. Stupid ass music played by crazy looking people, no, I do not want any parts of that Las Vegas entertainment. Save that for tourists and locals going on dates. How about I toss a tip to the kids dancing near the escalator outside of The Bellagio on Las Vegas BLVD; what I see from them is far more interesting and entertaining. Their jaunts and twists and turns and flips over one another, their charisma in getting the crowd involved in their show. It is a remarkable sight.

"Alright crowd! We need ya to clap...lets go clap," the leader of the crew would say, making sure that the crowd is paying attention. The group performed, bouncing off of the ground like rubber, launching themselves over other members of the group and throwing one another into the air, only for the human missiles to land gracefully on their feet. It was breathtaking and real.

Amidst the throng of people moving like a big ass worm up and down The Strip, a man dressed as The King is harassed by a group of white college students, three guys break dance wearing various U.S. President masks, and an old lady racks up dough in a shoe box because of her dancing American Bulldog. I've seen plenty of acts such as this in various parts of the country and I am always surprised by one thing; the blackness. I suppose its ok though, the money is tax free. I remember seeing a guy from some island while I visited Venice Beach, hop from a milk crate onto broken glass. I was shocked and amazed to see that none of the glass had penetrated the skin of his feet. The people in the crowd were even more shocked that the dread head man with three front teeth missing told them, "I don't do this for free," and collected his loot before he did his stunt. I was high as fuck, so I paid him no mind. You're not getting any money out of me for proving that you know how not to harm yourself. But, this is Las Vegas, and the energy is totally different. I was in awe of the spectacular display of colorful lights and shapes that I was witnessing while standing on Las Vegas Blvd, jacked up on acid. Every time one of the artists landed onto the pavement, a wave of energy of multi-colored lights would splash like paint into the air. The high flying acrobats looked like glow-sticks as they glided through the air with neon lights surrounding them. But how long could these intense waves last? I hoped not longer than eight hours because eventually I was sure to go crazy. Have you ever seen binary code? It's quite remarkable when you witness it developing on your cell phone screen, only to run off of the screen in a straight and never ending line.

"Yo, how long are we going to fucking stand here?" Corey chided. "I'm gonna walk back towards the room." He must have been getting irritable.

"Shut your ass up will ya... you see the guy is high as fucking shit," Melody flared. I felt someone tapping my shoulder, but my fascination with street acrobats transforming into pink and orange teddy bears was beginning to become a little too much for me, a little too real. A pull at my arm jolted me into a temporary sanity.

"I need a drink," I blurted. "We gotta find a bar. I need music. And more drugs."

Maybe this whole acid trip thing wasn't such a good idea. It alters reality in such a way that one really does seem maniacal to himself. Gigantic wasps flying overhead and tourists resembling dwarves, I just pray that I do not lose my cool. But, I suppose that I shouldn't want to be like a dinosaur. Because if I don't adapt to change then that is what I will become, and we all know what happened to the dinosaurs.

As we approached a mammoth casino, I witnessed three demons holding picket signs, screaming blasphemies.

"All of you will go to hell! The Lord will have his vengeance on your sins! You must face them!" they screamed, as vultures and honey bees floated around.

"Jesus reigns!"

Oh great, just what I didn't want to see...my stupid ass imagination and I, always presenting some type of demonic instance into my life. This isn't the bad part, however. The most horrific part of this scene is the fact that it is only beginning and will get much, much worse. Why do we have to walk past them? Why couldn't they be on the other side of the street? Hopefully they won't say anything to me, because as high as I am, I will react.

Fuck! Why does this have to be happening?

"Sherm," Shelby said, grabbing my arm.

"Fuck 'em, just keep it moving. We really don't have time."

Shelby has been witness to my behavior towards street evangelists before, however Corey and Melody aren't privy to my reactions.

"Alright bro," I said while giving my brother a twisted smile. His look was of disgust, behind the glowing lights blazing from each orifice on his face. I'm in Vegas. It's time for a fucking show.

"Hey gentlemen and lovely lady, can we talk to you about the Lord?" A blue eyed demon with red skin and horns coming from his forehead, dressed in khaki bell-bottoms and a multi-colored shirt asked as we walked by. I stopped in front of the demon as he handed over a brochure with "Heaven Wants You!?" across it. Heaven wants me? Well, who said I wanted Heaven? What is Heaven? Is Heaven some mythical land of unicorns and mermaids? Is it some place where all the good hearted dead people now reside? Is Heaven some special paradise where Jesus is sitting at the right hand of God while some arch angel stands at the pearly gates letting people in or banishes them to hell? Whatever Heaven is, I hope it is as free as Las Vegas. The things most people love are here in abundance. And a lot of love is Heaven, right?

"What's that scripture mean, to you?" I asked curiously, looking up at the sign that the blue eyed demon held. Corey and Shelby eyed me angrily, while Melody giggled. I'm beginning to like her.

"Well, yes. I do. Do you know what it means young man?" The demon asked, motioning over to his hideous cohorts. Their eyes gleamed green and on their glowing red skin you could see nasty warts oozing excrement with neon yellow gas steaming from them.

"Well, I fucking asked what it meant, not if. Didn't I?"

"Sherman! What in the fuck, you can't say that to these people!" Shelby screamed, causing bystanders to turn and look towards us. I glanced at Shelby and back to the creepy ass demon man with the blue eyes. Why in the hell can't I? What type of redundant reverse conversation is this thing attempting to have with me? He did solicit ME after all.

"I'm sorry for cursing, but you're the one that approached me as if I were a prostitute. Now, could you please explain to me what your sign means?" I asked, pointing into the sky at the sign that the demon so affectionately clutched.

"Well, its Jeremiah Chapter 1 Verse 5 and it sa...," the demon spouted, before I cut him off.

"Yes, I know demon man," I said. I looked around to see that Corey and Shelby had left the area, more than likely in search of booze. Melody stood to my left, a head full of multi-colored spaghetti noodles flowing down past her shoulders. I looked down and noticed that her shoes glowed bright red heels. Imagine coveted ruby red slippers, but in a 6-inch pump. The horror of beholding a flock of gigantic tropical birds that have surrounded and entrapped you with the three demons preaching the word of Christ is something that I do not wish on anyone. The glowing Las Vegas lights glared and the buildings loomed over us while stretching upwards into forever.

"I simply want to know what you think the sign means. Who knows, we may believe the same thing."

The blue eyed demon squinted and cocked his head, looking me over as if plotting what to do with my soul.

"Well, young man the scripture means that before God created Jeremiah in the womb, he already knew him to be set apart as a prophet for God. Does that answer your question?" The main demon spoke in a matter of fact tone, the other two snickering and giggling behind him.

"But what does it mean to you? Can I have your horns?"

The demon stepped back and eyed me again, this time puzzled.

"Well, it means to me that God also knew me before he formed me."

"Ok great me too, it was nice talking to you." I hooked my arm under Melody's and tugged. We must make a hasty exit from these demons. This is a pointless conversation. See, I'm no Jesus basher. I respect Jesus as a prophet. I respect Jesus as the son of God, in the same way that I respect myself as a son of God. I am made of the same stuff that Jesus was made of and that God is made of and that the Universe is made of. I am energy, period. Just like God and the universe, I cannot be created or destroyed. I can only be transferred to, from and through other energy. Plus, If God knew us before we were in the womb, then God also would have had to have known us before we were created into human form. If our existence began with God, then we have no foreseeable limits and can do remarkable and tremendous things. Like do what Jesus did, right?

"But young man I'd like to talk about why you are out here. What is it that you seek in this land of sin?

"Homie, what kind of question is that? This is Vegas. Fuck you doing out here?"

"No need to curse. What do you do for a living?"

"I'm an alcoholic, drug addict, and sex addict…fuck it, I'll just call it what it is. I'm addicted to avoiding reality," I said, leaning close to the devilish bastard. "Fuck you and fuck off."

The demon took a deep breath and large step back. "Jesus loves you, young man, Jesus loves you."

"Wait, what?! What do you mean Jesus loves me?" I yelled at the top of my lungs. Oh shit, I could feel something weird happening but I couldn't control myself. Was I going mad? I'd never tripped off acid. Why have I no couth? I stepped closer and grabbed his shoulder and asked with all earnest intent: "Did he say something to you? Oh man this is insane; Jesus told you he loves me? Really? Tell me his exact words!"

"You're going to hell young man! Repent in church young man, before it is too late. I seek Heaven; I seek the kingdom of God!"

I suppose the demon thought I was joking…and maybe I was. But I couldn't tell if I was or not. I was that off. Oh well, fuck it. Melody began tugging at my arm to walk away, but one of the minion demons cut her off. The crowd of tropical birds; parrots, colorful cranes, and hummingbirds buzzed and cackled with excitement. How in the hell did we end up getting in this predicament? It's quite ironic that demons are preaching to me about church. Maybe I should have listened to Shelby after all. Maybe I should have paid them no mind. My head began to pound and the sounds of chatter rose in my head so loud that I thought my ears were going to bleed. Snatching away from Melody, I turned to the blue eyed demon and stepped towards him.

"Look you motherfucker, there's a fucking church here. If I want to hear some Jesus freak talk, I'll fucking go there. Matter of fact, there's a church on every block in every hood in America. What the fuck good is that? Jesus built people, not churches."

"Ok, now I got ya," the blue eyed demon snarled. This must

be a game to him. "God knew you before you were born! He damned you to hell already!"

Melody burst into laughter and many of the birds in the crowd followed. A few of the vultures had joined the mix, I suppose to eat my rotting flesh after these demons crucified me on a neon sign. The acid bent my mind and I could not recognize what was real and what wasn't, yet laughter came out of me as well. It was infectious.

"This bitch is keeping it childish for the nine, nine and the two thousand ain't he?" Melody exclaimed, the crowd amused unbelievably. This is really odd I thought, birds laughing like humans. Acid is a hell of a drug.

"Sherm, come on let's go. The three stooges out here are lonely as hell. Cooperating with the good is just as important as not fucking with the evil shit. Let's go to the fucking bar!"

I grasped Melody's hand, and said to the blue eyed demon: "By the way, solicit is such a pretty word for prostitution. Keep it up. When I grow up all big and strong I want to really solicit. It sounds pretty, like someone doing ballet."

Melody and I turned our backs to the demons and as we walked hand in hand through the crowd of feathered laughing animals, we locked eyes.

"If you have sex with me, I promise I won't ask for your phone number."

A smile beamed across her face, a radiant orange glow as her spaghetti stringed hair swayed with her walk. I wonder what she looks like naked.

"I specialize in subtle hints and innuendo, sweetheart," Melody responded, dropping my hand and making a sprint for the door of The Bellagio. She can run in heels? Who does she think she is? I smiled and gave chase in the same manner a cheetah rampages after a gazelle, and thought about the old saying 'If you see a unicorn, hop on its back and tame it for yourself.'

"Only unicorns though," I yelled, "Not horses in disguise!"

~

The art of flourishment is something that many know nothing about. What is the art of flourishment, you ask? Is flourishment even a word? I'll take you back to the demon guy's bible scripture,

Jeremiah chapter 1 verse 5:

"I knew you before I formed you in your mother's womb. Before you were born I set you apart and appointed you as my prophet to the nations."

As aforementioned, if God knew us before he allowed us to be able to be created in the womb, then our existence began and begins with God. If our existence began with God, then our existence is limitless, because God is limitless. And if our existence began with God then it began as spirit. And if our existence began with spirit then it began as energy. And energy cannot be created or destroyed, only transferred to, through and from, just like God. What is the universe and stardust and all of that extra-terrestrial crap made of at its core? Energy...we are, in our purest essence, the same as the universe. We are also the same as a table, the same as a grain of sand, the same as the flight of an eagle even; Energy. Even our thoughts, the most magnificent attribute of a human-being due to our imagination, are energy. And this energy forms matter. If it were not for a thought, the seat you lounge in right now would not exist. It would not have even been THOUGHT of. Nothing has ever been created or innovated or much less done, if it were not for a thought. Thoughts must be matter, and by placing action and energy behind this matter, the idea begins to take shape and manifest itself into the material. I had an idea that I wanted to write this book. And hell, I fucking did. The fucking Presidents of the United States had the bright ideas of "Oh hell, I think I want to be President." 'I think' became 'I want' and 'I will'. It baffles me how atheists' and many other 'where's your God at now?' types will deny the belief that a God exists but make claims about the universe being in utter control and fate being something that no one can escape. A bunch of fucking spooks I tell you. Even if you were controlled by some parallel universe where there are a billion other yous living out different lives or even the same life with different circumstances, something has to be giving you the consciousness in the ONE life that you are conscious of. You are driving down the street, listening to top 40 music, enjoying the day that you are fucking leading. You're enjoying it so much so that you neglect to notice the child running into the middle of the street, chasing a ball. In one instance, you hit the kid and kill them, and keep going as if nothing ever happened. Thinking it was a dog or an over-weight cat, you continue on your way only to be arrested for the hit and run of a six-year-old. In another parallel, your vehicle came to a screeching halt, narrowly missing the child. You noticed the child and swerved out of the way in another parallel, hitting a tree and breaking your leg. Yet and still, in another parallel life you spotted the child well before hand and was able to halt your vehicle several seconds before the child ran into the street, getting praise from the parents of the child for your remarkable skill at paying attention to the road. Which one of these parallels do you experience however? The paramount experience is the one that you experience, in my unimportant opinion. It may totally depend on what you did earlier that day or that week or that month, but more than likely, the parallel that you were conscious of is the experience of coming to a screeching stop, narrowly missing the child. The parents are still happy that you noticed the child and are also slightly scolding to the child for being such a dumb ass to chase a ball into the street. These are both good experiences. You also tell yourself that you should pay more attention to your surroundings while driving because you almost crushed a poor child's head with your mini-van tire. The craziest thing about the universe is that it makes so much fucking sense that we think it makes no sense at all. Everything is literally everything, once we sit down and appreciate the wholeness that is. We experience ourselves, our thoughts, and our feelings separate from everyone and everything else, yet are infinitely connected with time and space. This drives us into an aberration of misled thought, entrapping us and binding us into a mental and spiritual slavery for manifesting our desires. This becomes a larger issue when our desires and our pursuit of these desires causes others happiness to deteriorate. We cling to our attachments; the people, places, things, our wants & desires. We must free ourselves from this selfish thinking, from the attachments that we hold that form the prisons that we inhabit. Embrace everything that is with life and the beauty of the natural order of everything and be compassionate to it. Serve others, love others. It is quite alright to desire things and people, however if it is not to serve or help others and to make them happy, then it is not sufficient enough to be considered all good, therefore diminishing the negative aspects of anything surrounding. Appreciate the stars and the Heavens and the water and the land and the grains of sand. Appreciate the blowing of the wind that moves pollen to and from. Ok, let's look at it this way…Once we recognize that we are simply spirit going through a human experience, we can see the beauty in living. Yet, we let our child-like state flee as we grow 'older', in the mold of something that isn't designed to live forever. Think, be a child, use your imagination and flourish. Don't be attached to any one thing, don't let it hurt you. Be, Bacon. Be the thing that makes someone else smile and I guarantee that you will smile. Be the thing that someone loves, even if it would kill them. We all know that everyone loves bacon.

FRIDAY, 7:00 A.M. PST

"What in the flying fuck are you doing man?" Corey asked, handing me a bottle of water. I take it, but stay lying on my back staring at the sky. My head is throbbing and I can barely make his face out. His voice is calming however. The sky is a beautiful hue of white, purple, blue, and orange and I instantly begin to wonder if I am still tripping off of the acid from last night. In my head it feels like someone turned the volume up entirely too loud. Why am I lying on my back in the grass, looking up at this beautiful sky? Where am I? I'm lying in the grass, looking up at the beautiful sky. I must have fallen down drunk, but that's not the point.

"Get the fuck up man."

I heard Shelby's voice. It seemed so close yet so far away. What in the hell did I do last night? The last thing I remember is running into Planet Hollywood and having a seat at the bar. Circus animals were running wild in the casino; monkeys swinging from the rafters, tigers sunbathing & elephants playing dominos. I remember wondering why in the hell they were playing dominos in a casino, but I didn't bother asking them.

"Where's the girl?" I muttered loosely. My face was numb.

"Sherm, man, come on," Shelby said as he waved his hand back and forth over my eyes. "Dude, you ain't blinking. Is that shit normal?"

"Who the fuck knows man. Let's get this asshole up before the cops see him, I'm surprised he lasted this long out here," Corey chided, obviously frustrated by my lack of reservation. "The motherfucker who insisted on us taking it slow the first night is the first one to die. How in the hell does that work?"

Corey and Shelby grabbed me under each arm and set me up, then lifted me to my feet. I gathered myself and gained my balance and commenced dusting myself off.

"Fuck you, I'm immortal," I said, to no one in particular.

"What in the fuck are you talking about?" Shelby asked with a disgusted look on his face.

"He's fucking bugging out man," Corey responded.

"By immortal, I mean I look like a fucking super hero. I would say that I am a god, but they're taking shots of gin right now," I said, wiping down my white dress shirt and black dress slacks. I love this fucking shirt. It's extra slim fit, straight from the manufacturers. I probably have stains all over it and I know that I probably look as bewildered as a mother that has lost its toddler in the supermarket. "It could just be the drugs though."

Shelby and Corey both shook their heads in disappointment. I looked at Shelby and noticed the intent look on his face. He's never been one to like it when I go missing and this is definitely a party foul. Everyone asks if he and I are twins, but I don't see it. I'm two years older, shorter and much more of a heathen than my younger brother. He has a tall and slender build and with his face lined with a beard, he resembles an east African. I've always been a little envious to the fact that he had facial hair well before me and is taller than me. I was relegated to needing Rogaine for beards and a booster seat.

Looking him up and down, I noticed that his white linen pants were ripped.

"What happened last night?"

"How in the hell should I know?" Shelby said angrily. "Nigga your fucking phone is off. We were looking for you all last night. We figured you'd meet us at the casino."

"Whoa, calm down compadre. You fuckers walked off and left me, knowing that I was high as fuck on drugs. Fuck y'all."

"Yeah Shelby, this is no worse than you waking up in the kiddie pool in your mom's backyard. Asshole woke up asking for beer." Corey mocked.

Now that was a crazy night. I was a 19-year-old sophomore in college and my parents decided upon the bright idea of sailing to Mexico on a cruise for their 18th wedding anniversary. I was living at an on-campus dormitory and didn't want to go to a college party full of musty older teens and young adults or sit in one of the numerous dorms on campus watching movies and playing video games. Brain-storming, I pondered upon an idea that provides much validity to the assertion that there are only two things ever-lasting. And human stupidity is one of them. Stupid cannot be halted. I commissioned 5 of my friends to invite at least two girls. If those girls invited friends, they had to be female, which would allow for me to invite one extra male per two extra females. The numbers didn't turn out right, but the ratio of vagina to penis was a cool 22 to 10, so it turned out perfect. Inviting 30 people into my mother's home wasn't the stupid idea. Neither was asking each of them to bring a drug or some type of alcohol. The stupidity didn't occur when we began playing HORSE for shots of liquor or when that game of HORSE was for articles of clothing. The stupidity didn't occur when we all decided to have a naked water balloon fight or when a few young women with large breasts rummaged through my father's garage and found a kiddie pool. The stupidity had nothing to do with the girls holding a naked wrestling contest or even the after math of the sex-capade held in each room of my mother's home. Horny fucking college kids I tell you. The stupidity in this event was allowing my then 17-year-old brother to consume enough alcohol to sedate a hog. I remember searching for him all of the next morning, only to find him lying outside in the backyard, belly up in the kiddie pool, pant and underwear-less with a used condom floating around his head. Weeks later we found out that Shelby had boned a girl that many considered to be the most gorgeous on campus. I was envious for a few days, but felt bad for the poor kid and pretty stupid because he didn't remember any of it and I'm the one that let him consume all of that alcohol. Some memories are meant, and that was one of them. However, still to this day Shelby says that when he sees her out, she blushes. And that's all fine and dandy, but I'm still thankful that he didn't drown himself. How would I explain to our mom that I let my under-age younger brother drown in six inches of sex water?

"Where's the girl? How did y'all find me?"

"She found us," Shelby said, shaking his head. "She told me to tell you that she got a phone call and had to report for flights. A whole flight crew came down with an STD and her crew was assigned to fill for them."

"Well isn't that just great. I'll never see the broad again. Damn it. No more acid for me man, that shit did something to me. I wonder how much liquor I drank," I bemoaned, reaching into my pockets to assess the damage that the night caused. Surprisingly all of my belongings were still intact and on me. I counted my cash and folded it back into my pocket and fingered my dead cell phone.

One thing I've learned in my decade of getting trashed is that the key to retracing your night is to send as many drunk texts to random people and take as many pictures and videos as possible. I have hard-wired my brain to automatically make my body use all of the juice on my phone. Whether I'm tweeting outrageous non-sense, sending foul text messages to my old flings, Instagramming terrible photographs of myself, or drunk dialing people, I will always be able to figure out what I did, said, and where I've been. This developed trait will surely come in handy.

"Where in the fuck did you all go?" I asked, looking back and forth from Corey to Shelby. There we we're, standing in the middle of an open lawn, with foliage and flowers all around. I could tell that we were at a hotel on Las Vegas Blvd by the sounds. Even at the break of dawn people were out and about, chattering.

"And what in the fuck happened to your pants?" I asked Shelby.

"Long story man. It's morning, I'm tired," Shelby began, visibly weary. I assumed that he hadn't been to sleep nor to the hotel to rejuvenate his self by way of sleep or cocaine, so it was imperative that we get him back to the hotel room so that he can recuperate.

"Let's go to the hotel. I need coke."

In silence, the three of us marched down Las Vegas Blvd, giving tourists the evil eye while they ate breakfast. Coming down from an extra-terrestrial high is the worst experience known to man but it also makes you into a man. When you are as happy as a molesting coach in a room full of pre-teen males and higher than Pluto, you've got to expect the inevitable come down that makes you as belligerent as an 86-year-old with one leg going through dialysis in a veteran's hospital, on angel dust. You want to kill someone, anyone...including yourself. I remember one such come down off of MDMA that made me want to commit suicide for two straight days. I grew stronger from that ordeal however and since then have been able to take on any drug and conquer any negative emotion that comes my way.

~

"What in the hell is in this bag anyway?" I asked as I lifted a black duffel bag the size of a Pomeranian.

Sitting in a chair situated in front of the large window in our hotel room, I placed the bag onto my lap and unzipped it. Neither of us had thought to open the bag in our absent-mindedness when we arrived, and I for one was eager to know its contents. Shelby and Corey were busy sitting at the table, breaking down cocaine and pouring drinks. Do they ever stop? My younger brother is really getting a crash course in death and resurrection. I wonder how he is going to go out; in a pool, the middle of the casino, a woman's vagina. He'll resurrect and be in a damned drunk tank. These two fuckers are going to be dead tonight, I'm sure of it. They'll have to keep guzzling alcohol and sniffing powder in order to stay awake. At least I had taken a short nap.

"Sure y'all don't want to take a quick breather? Both of you look horrible."

They both looked over and eyed me intensely. I guess they were still upset that I had gone missing for a few hours. Their gaze brought about a swift reminder that my iPhone had died. I've got to know what in the hell happened last night! I'm sure that I wasn't too belligerent due to the fact that I didn't awaken in a Clark County drunk tank.

"Yo, charge my phone please," I said. I reached into my pocket, tossing it towards Corey. He shook his head no and looked at me. I was tempted to hurl a derogatory "Fuck you" at him, but the bag of unknown shit is much more important. Just like you're never too old to throw random things in peoples shopping carts when they aren't looking, you're never too old to meddle in some shit that you have no business. Whose fucking bag was this anyway? I suppose that I should look at this moment as beautiful and perfect and embrace it. Hell, I may find a shit load of cash in this bag. Or more drugs. Or a gremlin. Hopefully it's not a gremlin. Why was the mean guy so upset about his luggage? If it was just clothes I am sure that he wouldn't have been that upset. And why in the fuck did Shelby take it in the first place? Cocaine will make you do some crazy things. Maybe he had x-ray vision. I'll just let the ride drive me through the chaos.

"Why in the fuck are you talking to yourself dude? What in the fuck is wrong with you? Do a fucking line...and drink this," Corey nagged.

Am I really talking to myself? Did I really say those thoughts out loud? What in the hell?

"Dude, I told you to take a fucking line. Here, drink this too motherfucker. You need it."

I set the duffel bag full of unidentified shit on the floor and rose from my chair, ambling over to where they were seated. How in the hell is this mother fucker giving me pointers on how to stay sane? Damn it, this is Las fucking Vegas. There is no such thing as sane! Is searching for Heaven sane? Fuck no! Yet, we are on our quest for it here in this decrepit city, the city of sin and turmoil, where anything that you wish is provided. I should be happy to be here however, and I am, so these two fuckers and their attitudes can kiss my fucking ass. I suppose that the most beautiful way to fully express and have others realize what is in the bowels of your heart is to show and feel gratitude.

"And I want my cut of that cash if you just so happen to find some in that bag, loud mouth," Shelby said while handing me a cup of alcohol."

"Thank you. Oh, prick's put ice in the shit this time too huh?" I asked, bent over the table with a rolled up hundred-dollar bill stuffed up my nose.

When we had gotten to the hotel earlier this morning, we stopped at the gift shop in the lobby before coming upstairs, purchasing more alcohol, juice, and cigars. While we were browsing the place, Shelby suggested that we wear suits tonight. I was surprised that the gift shop had such a wide selection of cigars. What is better in Las Vegas than alcohol, cocaine, cigars and prostitutes? Shelby probably won't go for the prostitutes, but I'm sure a stripper or ten will suffice for him. I won't be dealing with prostitutes either, but Corey may. I suppose that I should be happy and eager seeing as the most beautiful way to fully express yourself and have others realize what is in the bowels of your heart is to show and feel gratitude.

I inhaled one line and then another, while Shelby and Corey did the same. I closed my eyes and rolled them into the back of my head. I think my fucking nose is broken. I opened my eyes and quickly reached over Corey's back, snatching a few tissues to blow my nose. Am I the only person that looks at the mess that you just blew from your nose? From blood to boogers to the multiple colors of mucus, I always have to look. The same goes for wiping my ass as well. I think that everyone should see up close just what is coming out of their ass so that they know what to or what not to put into their mouths.

Shelby and Corey raised their heads from the table, stood, and walked past the bathroom to the hotel door.

"Meet us at the bar," Corey said as he opened the door.

"No showers? Dirty bastards." I responded as they exited, the door slamming loudly. I finished washing my hands, drying them on the hand towel hanging to the left of me. Turning around, I looked at the bathroom, equipped with a stand-up shower and whirlpool bathtub. It's beautiful, really. The shower is equipped with a specialized head and the toilet even has its own room. Quarantine the vomit and fecal matter, smart….and this high tech showerhead, it has got to be good for something other than massaging your muscles, sore from projectile vomiting and lifting glasses of alcohol high into the air. I walked back over to the table, got myself together, and exited the room. Fuck the bag.

Making my way to the bar, I was startled by the number of people running amuck in the casino. I found it ridiculous that on a Friday this early in the morning people are gambling and having drinks. Motherfuckers go to your hotel suites and brew your coffee, sip on your incidentals. But get the fuck out of my way before dawn, especially when I am disheveled with cocaine. I should have a caution sign stapled to my belly.

Eyeing my two roadies sitting at the bar with an older gentleman, I moseyed over to them. As I approached, Shelby turned and noticed me, and waved me down.

"Sherm! Yo, you've got to meet this old guy. This nigga is from the fucking stone ages plus he's witty as hell. This old motherfucker would be the king of twitter."

I took a seat in a bar stool to the left of the old man that didn't seem to be quite that old at all. He was dressed in a white seersucker suit with navy pin stripes and a panama hat with sandy brown moc toe penny loafers on his feet. A dapper man, he looked as if he was in his mid-50's and I was impressed. I wonder if this guy is as decadent and depraved as I am. There we sat left to right; Me, this dapper old guy, Shelby, and Corey. The air was thick with despicable vibes from people whose only desire while in Vegas was to cause as much havoc to the next man or woman as spiritually possible. Why else would people be gambling, drinking and hurling curse words on a random morning? We aren't here for the tourist attractions and stupid gymnast's spinning wheels and hanging off of rafters. No, we are here to disrupt the harmony in the universe…change the course of history, create the very fucking future that we want. Remember...bad decisions make good stories. Be conscious of what you feed your brain and who you associate yourself with, however, never doubt why you are around others. Embrace...Experience. Let the bad decisions of others help you to enhance your own.

Looking at the old man, I noticed his golden tanned skin. I wondered to myself his race, but my attention was diverted to his wrist that was adorned with the most beautiful time piece I'd ever laid eyes on.

"You like this garbage? It's over-priced for some gold bullshit, but I got it during a charity auction. Up-staging Chapo. Lord, luckily that's my daughter's husband."

"Man who the fuck is you and why the fuck is you talking to me about who the fuck you know?"

"I have nothing to hide young man," The dapper man said, his Spanish accent punctuated by a drawl. "I simply know something about you and was striking conversation. Blame your coked out friends for telling me about you."

I leaned forward and stared at Corey and Shelby with intent eyes.

"Bastards. Who in the fuck is this old guy?" I looked at the dapper old man again and noticed that his skin was golden and his hair was combed back with a light coat of gel. "You Cuban ain't you?"

He raised his watch to look at the time and the gold on it shone bright, momentarily blinding me like the sun does eyes that have relegated to darkness. His swagger tells it all...he feels like, me.

"Cuban?" The man said, raising his hand in the sky to motion the bartended over to us. "Yes, I am Cuban. How did you know this?"

"You look like it."

"My name is Santiago Mora. I am not Cuban, although I spent a great deal of time there the past 40 years. I am from Andalusia; it is a town in Spain. I enjoy your energy. You want a lot huh?"

"Man, I'm sorry...but I am high and with my family...and you, whom I just met, are really talking some deep ass shit to me. It's freaking me out."

"You can be open," he said.

"Open?"

"I have nothing to hide, as you do not. Stop being high and enjoy your conversation with me. You just might find what you are searching for," he said.

Leaning to the left, I squinted my eyes and wondered just what in the hell this guy was up to. Shelby and Corey hadn't mumbled a word, instead brewing over their drinks as if the tongues of both of them have been cut out by Medusa herself.

"The dog might die," Corey said, running his hand through his hair.

I gave Corey a shrewd look, my face wrinkled and ugly, as if someone farted and it smelled of sulfur and rotten eggs, "What in the fuck are you taking about? Dog?"

Corey looked at me bewildered. Wow? Really? How in the hell is he this fucked up, I hope this guy isn't dying.

"It's ok," the old man said in a soothing voice as if to calm me down. What does this guy want? It's like he is reading my mind and making me divulge information from myself without really giving much of anything out. "Karma is letting you off lightly because you're a new kind of crazy."

I looked at the guy with stoned eyes while he stared in return. I'm a decent man and have changed. This guy is ridiculous.

"Having demons is last year's issue old man and drugs are always cuddly and understanding. Take what you want from these words, but let us enjoy this morning and, buy my friends and I a few drinks."

Santiago looked at me with his pale blue eyes and smiled, and a sense of relief come over me instantaneously. How could this be? This random man, making me feel as at home as I have ever been. Suddenly the bartender popped up in front of us.

"Same old, Santi? Four?"

"Yes Jose. That will do. Sherman, do you enjoy writing?"

The fuck?! He knows my name as well…just great. These two blabber mouthed powder heads cannot seem to hold water. If their heads weren't attached by their necks, they wouldn't even have heads for crying out loud. It is remarkable that Shelby and Corey haven't whispered more than a few words. Are they in awe of this man? What could he have said to them before I came around? What could they have said to him before I was present? More than likely too much…I am glad that I never did much business with either of these two. Sure, Shelby and I sold several hundred pounds of mid-grade marijuana together and Corey and I have made a significantly strong bond over cocaine, however nothing was ever serious enough to the point that they would be pressured to speak on too much. This guy must be wired.

"Are you a cop?"

Shelby and Corey leaned back in their seats and gave me a face reminiscent of having entered a vagina rancid with an odor not even azithromycin could conquer. Santiago reared back and laughed swiftly, but didn't give an answer.

"Are you a cop?" I inquire, a bit sterner.

"Who taught you to say it twice?" Santiago probes, with a grin.

This motherfucker is really getting on my last nerve. He is so sarcastic and arrogant. He said that he was Italian however, so that would explain a great bit of it.

"I've been here quite a few times, Santi, and have met some pretty knowledgeable people."

"Dude, answer the fucking question. Sin told us that a few years ago. Stop talking in circles," Shelby says rudely.

"I could care less who the guy is, you fucking moron," I sat back in my chair and wonder how in the world I share DNA with this douche. Has he no couth?

"Well, yeah…" I hesitated.

I wonder if this guy is wearing a wire…I don't know half of who this fucker is. Could it be in his belt? Or maybe it's nestled in his silly little trilby hat he's wearing, snuggled slyly in the little bow on his hat.

"Who in the fuck are you?"

I wasn't too enthused to be talking to this man. Shelby wasn't too shy though and I trusted his judgment to a certain point, this being the threshold. I hadn't come out here to make any connections. I was just trying to have fun…Shelby hadn't hustled in years anyway, why in the fuck was he so hype on talking a bunch of high bullshit to this guy? Fucking piece of coked out shit. Blabbering and bullshitting.

"Sherm," Corey said. It is odd hearing his voice at this time. I looked at him with a side eye. Ignorance is bound to spew from his fucking shit hole of a mouth. "Why are you so dead on the inside? Some woman must have really hurt you."

"What?"

This guy is fucking blazed.

As if summoned to present himself on cue, Jose passed each of us a drink. He must've been slyly eavesdropping on our conversation, more than likely picking up audio for the CIA or DEA…I have never understood why people allow those assholes to run their lives. Sure, they can create a living hell but shit…fuck them.

Ever so gracefully sliding each drink to us from the opposite side of the bar one by one, like Olympic curlers slide those big ass blocks of what in the fuck ever over ice, Jose and his slicked hair was a sight to behold…All 5 feet 4 inches of him. I'll trust his drink making skills, because hell, he is all I have at the moment. I wonder what in the fuck is mixed with these drinks anyway. I was too busy being jumped by two hyenas to pay attention to what he had put into them. Hopefully I won't die from drinking it. Hopefully this shit takes these fools minds off of this bullshit they are speaking of.

"I have a real zombie fetish because of you now…because of how dead you are. Fuck you man," Corey joked.

"Sometimes kid, the broad that you so love, ain't gonna love you back," Santi said in a matter of fact tone, taking a sip of his drink. He even stuck his pinky out while drinking. "And there is no amount of duct tape or a trunk large enough to make her stay with you."

"I chase my liquor with liquor, bitch," Corey added, lurching toward me in a drunken stupor.

"Corey! Fuck you dude!" I couldn't take much more of the bullshit. How in the hell did I end up sitting here while two idiots and a random Cuban Spaniard chattered bullshit out of the side of their asses? Where in the fuck are all of these random ass statements and comments materializing from? Ignorance at its finest…I can't wait to get away from these two fucks.

"Sherm," The Spaniard called. Although I was tempted to rise from my chair, I refrained from doing so. "…perspective…it's limited by how much bullshit you know. Expand your knowledge, expand what you actually see. Your awareness, your insight. What really IS. Release your regret…."

Regret? What regret? Do you despise not being able to put the truth into something viewable? Or is it something different? Is it something that makes you simply get through it? Where is the breakthrough?

"I don't regret getting married very often, but when I do it's always," Santi speaks with vigor, as if he has wanted to say these words to an audience that would listen for a very long time. "Now-a-days man, I just get drunk. A lot of people bitch and complain. I just get drunk."

"That's nice old guy. But look...who are you?" I hadn't found out who in the hell this guy was. And then it hit me...The best is yet to come. It's going to get weirder.

"I just realized, I don't even like you for real," Shelby raised his head and looked at me, speaking this blaspheme as if it is as regular as an irregular t-shirt.

"Fuck you bitch, you're the piece of shit wearing ripped pants. How in the hell did that happen anyway?"

Shelby stood from his chair to reveal his mutilated pants. The rip in it seemingly larger than it had been when they found me in the bushes. What had this clown done to rip his pants in such fashion?

"Long story man," Shelby said as he pirouetted, showcasing the 12-inch rip from his crotch down to his left leg.

"Well Shelby scissor dick, you have absolutely nothing to do and all of the time in the world to do it," I said.

"His dumb ass fell in the damned bushes," Corey said before tossing back his drink and slamming his glass down on the bar. "Dumbass was stumbling all over the place and literally fell into a sea of Asian tourists. I've never seen a man be so ravaged by other men...they tried to rip him to shreds."

"You got into a fight Shelby?" I asked softly, the expression on my face clearly showing my confusion in what Corey just said.

"No," Shelby is short and stern.

"Man they attacked him. They thought he was an actor."

"I tried to run, but I slipped and fell into some bushes," Shelby sat back in his seat and shook his head. "Corey just laughed the whole time. Didn't even help me out of the bushes."

"Why would I help you out of the bushes that you decided to fall in?"

"Fuck you. A gang of midgets weren't chasing you," Shelby said.

"I would've given 'em some autographs," I said.

Shelby and Corey burst into laughter as I vomited words that really didn't matter.

"All of them look pretty much the same to me though, but then again all white people look alike too. Ain't that right Ronnie?"

"Yup...I'm giving out free tittie licks tonight man. We can't have a rerun of last night," Corey responded.

Santi sat in his chair, sipping from his glass while looking left to right as we spoke. As he sat and listened to us go back and forth, his smirk turned to a large grin. I've always held the notion that people who smile and laugh early in the morning are trying to cover up the fact that they are hiding dead bodies in the vicinity. Mornings are designed for remembering what in the hell happened last night and who it happened with, not jubilance and enthusiasm.

"Santi, you asked me if I enjoyed writing..." I said, while Corey leaned and grabbed the hat off of Santiago's head. This guy is really something else. Corey is due to crash and burn soon. I'm sure of it.

"Where'd you find this guy?" Santi said to me, visibly perplexed. "It's like he's a wild animal."

"Hell, he found you," I glanced back to Corey and saw him pull his cellphone out of his pocket, which reminded me that mine was still in the room. I wonder what in the hell I did last night. Corey began taking pictures of himself; an odd sight to see any grown man doing in public. It is an incredibly suspicious act to behold in its purest form, when a grown man fills his cellular phone camera roll with 25 pictures of his face, choosing one to post to a social media website. Can you imagine the type of helpful shit that we could do if we endowed others with our time instead of taking pictures of ourselves? The world would no longer be dark and destruction worthy, I am sure of it. Absolutely...yes, we'd easily stamp out poverty and create so much peace in the world that everyone will bask in the glory of their awesomeness. Everyone would appreciate every day that the good Lord gives them...

"Selfie!" yelled Corey, his voice reverberating through what seemed like the entire casino. And nobody paid any attention. Such is life in Las Vegas.

Corey has the insane ability to prove me right at the perfect times. His actions always seem spontaneous, but I know better than to believe that they aren't premeditated. He prefers to make a person think that he is as incompetent as a toddler is studying algorithms of the gamma wavelengths between Sirius B and Earth. Preference is the captain of many people. It's so odd to me, how things are geared towards preference. Preference is ridiculous as the wind. It's the same as the emotion of a woman; here, there, fleeting and embracing. You can wake up out of your slumber on a random Saturday morning and prefer to eat cereal instead of pancakes. The next Saturday, instead of cereal, you prefer steak and eggs. Even still, the next week you may prefer pancakes over waffles. Preference is simply put, a stupid word for the ability to change your fucking mind. Everybody does it, young and old. Men prefer a certain type of woman when they are young and maybe when they get older they'll prefer a different type of woman. Someone prefers a certain type of drug one day and ten months later prefers a totally different drug. It's commonplace for human beings to change their attitudes and their preferences, but is it commonplace for humans to change their behavior? Fuck no. Yes, some people do change their behavior...from smoking to not smoking, from drinking to not drinking, from not exercising to exercising...but the majority do not. Most people are creatures of habit. Once we get in the habit of doing something, we continue to do the essential functions of the habit. We may change our preference of how we go about succumbing to habit, but we still succumb to habit. A motherfucker is going to get high. Whether a real deal junkie has to do crack, heroin or crystal meth, the poor bastard is going to get his fix. A motherfucker could love cars just as much as that fiend loves dope, purchasing vehicles on whims because he "liked it at the time". Sitting in front of a fucking television, the right wealthy motherfucker might see four or five commercials of different vehicles and change his mind so many times that he buys one of each vehicle he saw during commercial breaks for the Super Bowl. Behavior is the true culprit. If you want to really solve something, change the behavior behind it. You want someone to stop smoking? Don't give him an alternative, such as electronic cigarettes or hookahs. The fact remains, the bastard is still smoking something. Now, if you want to change a specific behavior, such as smoking tobacco ...what needs to happen? ...A change in attitude, a behavior change, or both?

This is all a part of my unimportant opinion of course...but it goes to show that low-risk people will follow protocol through policy change and high-risk people will indeed rebuke policy, needing a change in behavior. My opinion is unimportant, and I shan't offer any ways to people to succeed, but who gives a shit. No, I do not want watered down and ignorant people that do not care about their community or the uplifting of their community. We must change behavior, as a people.

As a whole, we must change the perception that the world has of us. Yes, the world enjoys everything black. Black clothes, black music, black women, black lipstick, blackberries...man, motherfuckers love black. How can you hate black skin yet love what blacks offer and have given to the world? If we start with ourselves and change our behavior...we don't have to go back to the 'we shall overcome' gung-ho rhetoric that ushered us into this space. We don't have to go back to the 'by any means necessary' mantra either. We don't have to believe in supporting ONLY black business, because hell, all of the civil rights motherfuckers fought for a nigga to be able to go anywhere I please, so by God I certainly shall.

That is one thing I have never understood and maybe it is the alcohol or the drugs, but why on earth would people fight for desegregation only to say fifty years later "we need to support our own black businesses" ...No shit asshole.

That's neither here nor there however and I'll refrain from offering my full opinion on something that I absolutely know as less as anyone about. The key is to change our behavior. We don't have to be timid. We don't have to be afraid. However, we do need to be God-honest citizens that live happily. Instead of robbing and thieving, maybe we should be patient and work hard. The people who have made it out of the hood shouldn't act as political democrats do. They should not come back and give repeatedly, creating dependence upon their donations. They tell us to act ignorant and give us tales of activity that they are currently not engaged in. It is a perpetual cycle of profiting off of another s misfortune. They should come back and teach, revitalize and, offer up hope in the form of education. Fuck your schooling, how about you educate me in how to be self-made. Educate me on how to truly be a benefactor of my own Self. Education comes from within.

Is it reasonable to fear a black male, young or old? A large part of the hip hop culture would tell you to, as braggadocios tales of dope dealing and murder reverberate through speakers. If we changed our behavior, starting from the people that influence the bottom rung citizens, society will begin to change. It must be a grand collaborative effort. Black mothers, stop the perpetual devaluing of your black sons…. "Niggas ain't shit." If you tell us that we are not shit, we will act like we are not shit, and you cannot be upset when the outside world treats us as if we are not equivalent to shit.

"You should probably write that down kid," Santi said as he finished his drink.

What? Had I gone on a tangent while sitting here? What drug induced and alcohol driven words did I speak? What angst did I show? I looked to my right and noticed Shelby and Corey giving me a feverish look.

"What does that mean?" Corey asked hesitantly.

"Hell if I know. I'm about to go to sleep though man," I replied. I rose from my seat, embarrassed, and started to walk away when Santi called to me.

"Hold one second, kid. Here's a card," Santi said, rising from his chair. He reached into his pocket and pulled out a golden card, with white lettering across it. "Call me around 8. Get some rest. Dinner tonight, with Heaven. Wear a suit."

Heaven? What is this that this man spoke of? Yes, we were searching for Heaven in Las Vegas and by damn I think that we may have found it. When you really want something, the whole entire universe conspires to get it for you. I took the card from Santi's hand and walked away, not bothering to look back. I'll catch up with those two clowns later. The trek to my hotel room was a lonely one. Everything in me is closed, and the late night is no more. My only company was a gold business card with few words written on it.

Santiago Mora 702 - 567-7890.

FRIDAY, 9:00 P.M. PST

As the doors of the glass elevator opened to a large restaurant at the top of the replicated Eiffel tower located on Las Vegas Blvd, we were greeted by a Caucasian man dressed in a black tuxedo. Without speaking, he shook the three of our hands, turned, and motioned for us to follow. Stepping out of the elevator, I began to survey my surroundings. The amount of cocaine that we had just vacuumed on the ride to the top of the tower was enough to make an emaciated persons heart burst, and my senses were heightened like those of a super hero...or mad pit-bull. The restaurant was a lovely place with lovely décor and lovely atmosphere; glass chandeliers hung high in the air like snowflakes, each with their own unique design, with hanging plants adorning them, creating a sight that I had only imagined before. Stunning displays of flowers and candles set on each table creating a spectacle fit for aristocracy. The room resembled what I envisioned the palace dining rooms of Babylon to be; gorgeous and provocative, unique and non-traditional. The walls were even crawling with vines and flowers...beautiful flowers of yellow and pink and red and white, the light from the chandeliers reflecting so perfectly off of their hue that they danced on the faces of every guest. As I looked around, I noticed that not a seat was empty in the entire room, nor was a frown on any face. Why on earth is no one frowning? Not even the old geezer of a billionaire seated near the stage, next to his mistress and her new boyfriend. Everyone seemed to hold some sort of esteem. If you were here, you were SUPPOSED to be here. I couldn't spot a man that didn't have on a suit, nor a woman not in an expensive cocktail dress. What is a suit, though? Does a suit guarantee importance? Hell no, but it does make you look as such.

The air was thick with the smell of delectable food and sounds of jubilation and I would have believed that I was on the infamous cruise ship, Titanic, if it weren't for the beautifully lit stage to our left that held a band dressed in garb reminiscent of the 1960's performing Biggie Pritchards classic, "Little Old Annie". My only hope is that this building does not face the same fate as that doomed ship.

One of the reasons that I enjoy Las Vegas as much as I do is because everything is a caricature. I enjoy the fact that people are paid to mimic some of the most influential people that have ever walked this earth. It is captivating and enchanting to witness an individual's bliss as they imitate. They are here, if only for that reason. But why am I here? What is the purpose for my manifestation in this frequency? I'm a writer. A future doctor of communication. And I believe in the power of prognostic wisdom. Hunches, signs; be aware of them and take heed. I am searching for Heaven. And in my search, I know that only one thing is tried and true...the universe is going to give me what I want.

Attempting to people-watch while maneuvering through a restaurant and also keeping an eye on Corey and Shelby is more difficult than I had previously imagined, so I allowed the attention that I had set on them to be abandoned and faced the gloomy realization that we may not make it out of this place alive. We sauntered slowly, a difficult task due to my brains desire to engage my legs in bi-pedal locomotion, however it gave me a chance to become intimate with the energy versing through the room. It was alive and bright. The chandeliers that hung above each table glowed brightly, yet those in the rafters, the ones that gave the room its Heavenly radiance, began to diminish as we moved from the entrance of the restaurant to the back of it. The little person controlling my movements whispered something so faintly that I almost did not hear him, and I began to feel like I was walking through a gust of evil wind. In the shadows of the rear of the restaurant, nearly parallel to the stage, we strolled into a private room that reeked of the wretched and of the despicable. The infinite energy of joy and happiness that surrounded us upon our initial step out of the elevator had been replaced by the stench of self-loathing. In the rear of the room, four men sat staring at us, the table positioned horizontally along the wall so that they could see everything that entered into the room. I entered behind the host, with Corey and Shelby following, and was instantly bum-rushed by a grizzly bear of a gorilla.

"Drop the bag you little piece of shit, who in the fuck do you think you are!" roared from the bouncer's mouth. Regaining my balance, I stood. Unafraid...partly because of the cocaine but mostly because the voice sounded familiar.

"Pedro!" I ejaculated, anger jetting through me as I tried to remain clenched to the small duffle bag in my grasp. This bag, the same bag that was stolen from the airport by two nincompoops, was worth a hell of a lot more than we had bargained for, and it was the main reason why I believed that making it out of this building alive would be a tall task.

After we had ventured back to our rooms from our initial encounter with Santiago, I opened the bag that sat on Shelby and I's hotel room floor and was utterly astonished by what was found in it. An orgasm after 10 years of celibacy couldn't compare to the feeling that welled inside of me. I screamed bloody fucking murder.

Speaking to Santiago later in the day led me to briefly explain that I was in possession of an extremely valuable lot of items that he may be interested in purchasing. He laughed heartily on the opposite end of the receiver and I fancied him to be sitting near a pool with three 38D brunette beauties and a seductive red head feeding him grapes. He was pleasant, and told me to bring whatever I had to him and he would see what he could do.

"My name ain't no got damned Pedro, the fuck is you?!" Pedro yelled.

"Nigga it's your cousin! Sherm!" I yelled while being lifted three feet off of the ground, Pedro's grizzly bear gorilla claw hands grasping underneath my arms. This must be what a child feels like while being catapulted into the air. He could easily toss me through the ceiling. This was not a pleasant feeling. Simply put, it was a bullshit experience…. Why do we torture children with this horseplay? Raising them into the air, tossing them around as if they are rag dolls, even pitching them back and forth from one person to the next. Children cannot possibly think that this kind of treatment is fun, yet they laugh and giggle as if someone is tickling the bottoms of their feet. Repugnant.

"Pedro, you stupid motherfucker. I'm calling Aunt Pearly!"

Without warning Pedro dropped me and I fell twenty feet from the air, eyes winced and face wound tight, braced for impact. I wasn't lucky enough to break an ankle or femur, however.

"Holy shit. Why are you here?" Pedro's menacing eyes shot a hole through me. "And motherfucker what's in the got damned bag!"

"I don't get your point and I'll never get your point while you yell. Yelling is useless and you will never get your point across by doing so. Unless you have a gun. Now let us sit down."

Corey, Shelby and the male maid stood near, faces wrought with confusion as they witnessed sophisticated belligerence. They watched Pedro whip out a chrome .44 magnum from a waist belt holster and they gazed in wonderment as I told him that he was mighty handsome with his squirt gun and over-sized suit.

"Aunt Pearly still has that picture of you holding the pink squirt gun in your Easter outfit hanging in her living room. You dressed better as a child."

"Fuck you. This is my job."

"Nigga you don't work!" I laughed and dropped the bag onto the floor. I kneeled slowly and unzipped the bag, keeping an eye on Pedro and his .44 magnum. A nervous slip of his finger and I'd have a hole the size of a beer can in my head.

"Shut it," Pedro said.

"Thanks asshole," I said, rising from my position. "Nigga, you gotta be retarded as hell to pull a fucking gun on me. It's more in this bag than your fucking life would be worth a million times over. Fuck your job prick. I swear to god I'm telling auntie. Fuck you."

Since a child, I've wanted to be much more than a simple human. I never quite got there, yet the feeling that I get when on cocaine has enabled me to feel like it. It is wondrous, when one can simply do anything that he sets his mind to. Fear is none, especially when enraged. As I stood toe to toe staring creepily into the eyes of a brute, I came to the realization that I was not amused; he yearned-for expiration and I wanted to make sure that he never breathed again. In this very instance the universe provided us with the positioning on the celestial axis to be completely complimentary to one another. The love that families share is sometimes overshadowed by a bloodlust so bold that it makes vampires seem like gummi bears.

Showdown. Who's going to blink first? We stared at each other stupidly.

Shelby, Corey and the man-maid stood in their hallowed corner reciting the Lord's Prayer....Well, maybe not...however, in my mind they were therefore they were. The anxiety that came with looking into Pedro's eyes was swift and multiplied in such a way that it forced me to look away from him and to my comrades. So far so good, I thought. What had I done to deserve this? These two imbeciles had not a care in the world...stuck, as deer in headlights would be before it is ran over by a hapless hillbilly driving recklessly on an eastern Kentucky back road. Their faces weren't faces of fear but of worry, fore they understood the magnitude of the situation that we were in. Yet, I had the innate feeling that everything would be alright. Even if I didn't know when.

With bag in tow, I turned and walked towards the dinner table that the four men were seated at. The arrangement of the table was odd to the uninitiated eye, and uninitiated I certainly was. Santiago sat directly in the middle of the table, two people to the right of him and one to the left. The chairs across them in which we sat were orientated to sit opposite the spaces between the host chairs. It was an odd set-up, yet my brain was moving at such a rate that the issue of seat placement was cast-away.

We each took our turns sitting, minus the man-maid of course, Shelby to my left and Corey to my right. I placed the duffle bag underneath my seat and lifted its front right leg inside the hoop of one of the handles. No one was slipping this bag or its contents away from me. As we sat, Santiago stared, casually slouched with a cigar in his mouth, challis' full of a brown liquor in his grasp.

I've always been privy to the belief that I do not drink alcohol, but properly distilled spirits. Therein, I cannot become an alcoholic, I can only be spiritual. I was reminded of this by the radiant glow that Santiago gave off as he relaxed in his chair. He resembled a fisherman reposed on a West Indian beach sipping coconut water; majestic.

"Hasn't your mother ever told you not to slouch?" I wonder out loud in Santiago's direction. He didn't respond verbally, yet his reaction was profound. Raising upright in his chair, he tapped his cigar in a glass tray that glittered as candle light danced against it. With his left hand he raised his glass, bowing his head towards me in a gesture of goodwill.

"You're a feisty motherfucker aren't you?" a man with cornrows asked, leaning his head inquisitively. I didn't respond.

It was four of them sitting there, menacing and evil, a dark cloud of disgrace hovering over them. I had no idea what I had gotten myself into and with stress levels high, it was difficult to make the right decisions. I suppose I shan't care at all, tis but a dream in Las Vegas anyway.

Pedro stood near the entrance staring outwards towards the crowd. I wonder how he felt. Well, on second thought...fuck him.

There are certain ways that one is supposed to treat family, regardless of a bullshit job. What had he become here? It was a piece of shit transparency of who he had become and in a larger sense, what he had become. Brainwashed. Similar to those people who get caught in bogus drug stash raids. I find it hilarious that the Feds are being ridiculed by judges due to their use of ludicrous entrapment...It would seem as if the United States has been exposed as the detriment to its civilians that many of us have known for decades.

"Gentlemen," Santiago jolted. He sat his glass down to push his fingers through his white hair. "Business has begun."

"I thought we were just talking and eating. What kind of business do we have besides that?" I asked.

"My friends, let me introduce you to MY friends," Santiago stated as he pushed away from the table and stood behind the man on his left.

"Gentlemen, this is Geronimo," placing both of his hands on the braided man's shoulders. He held the appearance of a youth with the hard features of someone that had once been an impairment to society. A man of 32 or 33 years old with as much facial hair as a fifth grader, I pondered upon him briefly before noticing a red basketball on his forearm as he rested it on the table. His arms were littered with a number of ill-placed and unintelligible pieces of art yet this one stood out from the rest. He must play basketball. Why is he in Las Vegas of all places?

Moving away from Geronimo, Santi stood between the two men seated to his right, placing a hand on each of their inside shoulders.

"This is Primetime," Santi said as he looked left and then right, his face gleaming. "And this is Robbie."

He moved towards his chair to sit and puffed his chest in admiration.

"These men, including myself, are Heaven. We are what you have been searching for....and during this conversation, you will begin to understand why you have been chosen to meet Heaven. Understand, you will learn everything. I will begin by saying that I and the men sitting in front of you have nothing to hide therefore you also have nothing to fear. We are here to help one another. The bag that you all lifted from the airport belonged to Primetime," Santi stated.

My blood began to boil as Primetime stared a hole into each of us as if he had six eyes. I turned to Corey who was sweating profusely, his face and neck red from embarrassment or the threat of eminent death.

"Loooook, man. All of the chips are...," Corey began before being cut off mid-sentence by Primetime.

"Kid, if we wanted to kill you I would have done it at the airport. You and your high ass friend ran in a straight goddamn line," Primetime responded.

"Oh so that was you who said the N word. Not cool, bro," replied Corey.

"I'm not your bro. And I said 'lucky I don't pull the trigger'. I didn't say that, asshole."

"Two white men arguing. How cute," Geronimo butted in, ending their verbal tussle.

Primetime was of Irish decent, his strawberry blond hair cut similar to Santi's although it was not as long. A freshly groomed beard covered his strong jawline, giving him the appearance of a man much younger than his actual age.

"Gentlemen," Santi began. "Be amused. Be merry. And be eager to learn. The bag was supplanted to be seen and taken by you three. Corey, did you not see Primetime un-zip it on the plane?"

Shelby and I looked to Corey bewildered. How had the two of us not seen it? How? Corey was seated on the end; I suppose he caught a glimpse that no one else did. The sly devil.

"And Sherman, were you not intrigued by the woman suggesting you find Heaven?"

I should have known. A flight attendant would never let us use our tray boards as a surface to do cocaine off of...it's not like it was her boob or ass cheek.

Who were these men? Why had they chosen us? Only time will tell the outcome for us as we deteriorate in this decrepit town.

"I have come into contact with a group of very powerful men, these men are like me to you," Santiago cheerfully continued. "The chips? Yours. To share of course. My friends will be arriving shortly."

I sat, baffled and amazed at the complexity of the situation that we were in. Set up and brought here, seemingly on purpose. What pained me more than anything was that Melody was in on this illusion. Had we been kidnapped? How could I be so stupid as to not sense this? She was too good to be true. Even though I may not remember our night, I have seen the pictures, and I am sure that the way I feel, right now, knowing this…is how I should feel. Or maybe what I feel for her was nothing more than a hard-on of the heart; something new to jolt my spirit.

I remember Shelby had mentioned Santiago as being the man that I should talk too. The thought caused a rush of heat to come over my body and sent me into a dizzy spell that made my skin prickle. I became hot and began sweating from my forehead and underneath my arms. My suit was uncomfortable so I removed my jacket and unbuttoned the top of my shirt. I felt the sweat from the back of my neck soak my collar, and I could feel the sweat penetrating my white shirt; under the arms, along my spine and small of my back and even my chest area: In five seconds I had transformed from a well-coked machine into a slob wallowing in his own perspiration.

I'm sure that everyone had noticed how flustered I had become yet I could give a shit less. Their view of my image was much less important to me than my own view of reality was, yet I knew that this was totally wrong and I was totally fucked. One cannot, must not and may not seem like a cowardice puppy indulging in the practice of fearfulness in the face of men such as these. In the society that I enjoy frolicking through with reckless abandon…in the society that has allowed me to find Heaven in the faces of devils and demons in the land of deceit and debauchery…the way that I present myself in the face of wolves and lions is paramount to anything else. **Eat or be eaten, kill or be killed.**

Santi raised his hand and motioned a butler towards the table. Leaning to his ear, Santi whispered into it and the butler swiftly left the room.

"Sherman, no need to be nervous. Nothing shall happen. These men that we are set to meet are new to me and I would like to aide in your quest to be a writer of great impact to society. They were the ones, not I….not us," Santi said, gesturing towards the rest of Heaven, "that wanted you. They simply asked us to get you here. Primetime and Melody did a wonderful job."

"It's ok kids, we wanna know what these fucks want. And why they want you. They want your help," Robbie chimed in with a smile on his face. He hadn't spoken until now. His voice was pleasant and he beamed large white teeth towards me which instantly made me feel at ease. An odd thing it was, this man that could very much be a killer, easing my worries so that I had not a fear of being killed.

"Ya'll should loosen up," Robbie continued, eying the three of us. "Want a line?"

As perplexed by this question as I was, I had no intention of turning him down. I couldn't. Even if I had the desire to say no, my brain would force my body to take hold of the plate that Robbie had pulled out of thin air. A mountain it was; the pile of dope Robbie brought forth from underneath the table. I glanced at Corey, his eyes wide and glowing brightly. I figured the kook was less amazed by the drug and more vexed by the randomness and ease that it was offered.

"May I?" Corey muttered, reaching for the plate.

Robbie smiled and nudged it into his extended fingertips.

Grabbing the butter knife sitting next to him, Corey played in the cocaine as if it were a mound of mash potatoes. In an instant he had turned into a toddler, visibly fascinated by the shimmer of blow underneath the restaurant lights. Drugs bring everyone together in the grand scheme of things. Hell, without drugs we would all be docile and sedated creatures hell-bent on saving humanity from themselves. And no one in their right minds desires to be a prude being that has no communicative prowess. Everyone has something to say. Every single last one of us on this earth.

And that is the point. What we have to say, is what we have to teach. Each of us has something to teach the world, the universe, each other. And most importantly ourselves. It's fucking incredible.

"Hell motherfucking yeah man," Corey cheered, wiggling the tip of the knife into the mound. He pulled back a generous amount and cautiously brought it to his nose. He snorted it, gently.

"You got your kid gloves on today don't you motherfucker" Robbie jeered, snatching the plate from Corey.

Robbie then created a two-inch line for himself and leaned his face into the plate.

"Pussy. Your line looks like an inch-worm," Corey chided as Robbie inhaled his dope. Swift and clean, how it's supposed to be. Corey knows this. He's also as high as I have ever seen him.

"Fuck you," Robbie laughed, his voice loud and boisterous.

He looked towards Primetime and Santi, "You motherfuckers know something?"

"What asshole?" Primetime replied, visibly annoyed by Lord knows what. I could tell that Primetime had a ferocious temper, even though he seemed as docile as a puppy.

"Fuck, or fucking, it's probably the best word ever invented in the American language," Robbie said.

"We speak English, asshole," replied Primetime.

"Oh look what we have here, an Irishman saying that we speak English. How fucking funny."

"Fuck you prick," Primetime said. He rolled his eyes at Robbie and gave him the middle finger. "It is English."

"Actually no in the fuck it's not," blurted Shelby.

I thought the kid was dead honestly, he hadn't spoken a word damn near the whole time we've been seated. My younger brother is a sneaky person...many people are like this however. They don't mean to be sneaky. They are calculating to the point of existentialism, willing their way through life. I'm the same way, as are most people who have resilience and patience, however the gift of uncertainty is of the finest substance known to man, especially since whatever you want to happen will happen.

"It's fucking American and it's the best fucking word that you could ever use. It's a god damned noun, adjective, verb, adverb, pronoun and preposition. So fuck you, you fucking motherfucker and pass me the fucking cocaine," Shelby said.

We all burst into laughter, even Santi, who sat with his challis' in his hand. His shoulders bounced up and down as he chuckled heartily, amused at the banter that we partook in. I began to feel at ease as we sat, especially since Santi had relaxed. When the leader of a group of individuals is at ease and not agitated, the air in the area is lighter. Spirits lift that much higher and joy and happiness is able to creep its way into everyone. It is fact that the happiness of our own lives lies in the hands of our own selves. You will get your own happiness.

As the time passed, liquor poured and an immense amount of cocaine was inhaled. We became comfortable with one another. The waiter that Santi had summoned off had come back long ago with challis' for Corey, Shelby and I, and kept our glasses cold with a continuous flow of bourbon over ice.

As we sat snorting a mound of dope, each man told intimate

stories of themselves and their mishaps. The mishaps, these treacherous acts committed by or against each one of them were events that changed the courses of their lives from snug to ill-fitting. They didn't feel like mishaps to me however. No, they were something much more sinister and diabolical...these mishaps that each man spoke of were tools that enabled them to become what and who they were. The darkness that they delved into forced them to burn brighter and beam powerfully, slicing the darkness that surrounded them with their brilliant rays.

If it weren't for Geronimo's numerous run-ins with the law as a college basketball phenom, he may have very well been an NBA All-Star, perhaps relegated to the bench after a freak PCL injury sustained while jogging backwards after spectacular play. The irony of this scenario is that it did indeed happen, one month after a marijuana deal busted by the DEA was washed under the radar during his sophomore year of college. Playing against a conference rival team whose best player couldn't start JV for the local rec league, Geronimo made these young men seem like toddlers against a God. Yet, as fate would have it or as the real man on high had intended, after a windmill dunk and subsequent jeering of the home crowd, arms raised in triumph and jogging backwards to defense...snap...and on the floor the young man was. His PCL had torn in two places, a remarkable and never before seen injury as told by the surgeon. Weeks later his case leaked to the media; A sleazy and slimy expose featured on national news. Sports and Your Life broke the coverage, as customary in this new millennium, and the downfall of Geronimo commenced.

Here he sat, a man now committed to community development that was born to sell dope and not hope. How had his life turned out? Is it worse than what it would have been if he had played professional ball instead of prison league? Money was not an issue; I am sure of it. So is the road of tribulation; he has become something god-like on earth, seated as a member of Heaven. Humility in the face of pure ignorance, he was who he was destined to be in his own life's entirety.

"Rule number one," Santiago spoke while scrapping a line of coke together, "Pay yourself. First and foremost, always pay yourself. I want to teach you how to grow wealth and remain wealthy. You motherfuckers don't know shit about wealth."

"We don't know shit about wealth, but we know a goddamn

lot about some motherfucking drugs," Shelby yelped. "Pass the coke."

Robbie and Primetime's energy from their laughter surged through the table, and brought forth a jubilant expression that included numerous slaps against the table.

The mood had lightened tremendously and cocaine had been the catalyst for it. In Heaven, full of greed and lies and mayhem, Dope IS Hope.

Passing the tray to Shelby, Santi began speaking with vigor, "One must always pay themselves first young nig.."

"Cause if you don't, you're pretty much dicking yourself," Primetime spewed, cutting Santi off.

"The second rule is when you pay yourself, don't spend the shit. I blew my first million on a boat and prime real estate. They were great investments, except my prime real estate was built on a swamp in Louisiana," said Robbie.

"The dumb fucker didn't get any insurance," joked Santi, leaning down to the floor to tie his shoe.

"Fuck you," growled Primetime, snatching the plate from Shelby in the process. "I fucked up. I talked to a goddamned night club owner about real estate."

Santi continued to giggle as he rose from tying his shoe before looking me squarely in the eyes with a bright smile on his face.

"And that my friends, is the third rule... Don't listen to ignoramuses. A club owner... Jesus Christ."

"That motherfucker got what came to him for that dumb call too," Robbie chided, mincing his face at Primetime. "You're a shit head. It was your fault for listening"

"Fuck you Robbie. He shouldn't have lied," fired Primetime.

"He didn't fucking lie," Robbie returned.

"He did!" Primetime yelled and pounded his fists on the table. "And I shot the shit out of that motherfucker and put him in the god damned swamp with my real estate."

Shelby and Corey turned to one another with raised brows. I laughed as Primetime leaned away from the table and into his seat back. He crossed his legs and grasped his knee with clasped hands, staring at me as a dog would its owner when confused.

"What's so funny? You a murderer or something?" Primetime asked.

"No," I said replied nonchalantly. "I just think you're fucking stupid."

"The fuck you mean, I'm stupid? How am I stupid for making a bad investment?" replied Primetime. His shoulders relaxed.

Laughter erupted from around the table, causing a sonic boom of sound that I thought may bring the chandeliers of the entire restaurant down. Santi sat quietly however, purveying Heaven and his newfound comrades as a king would do his loyal subjects whilst set on his throne.

"Dumb ass," Geronimo chuckled. "You answered your own question."

We continued to laugh while Primetime rewarded us with fuck you's and middle fingers.

"Okay ladies," Santi interjected, his face which once beamed a glowing grin of playfulness now displayed a twisted grimace projecting discontent and malevolence. "Shut the fuck up."

Disputing philosophical concepts with a murdering drug dealer is the same as playing badminton with a chainsaw and I suppose that Santi understood this about Primetime.

"Santi, you act like I committed 14 murders because of an occult or some shit," Primetime said.

"No, I'm acting like the guy that gave you 25 grand to kill a motherfucker and you accepted 26 grand from him so he wouldn't kill you." Santi replied. His face had turned from golden to red, and I thought that he may have a stroke any second.

"But I killed him anyway, Santi!" Primetime rejoiced, throwing his hands into the air and cackling at Santi. Santi closed his eyes and shook his head in silent frustration.

"Y'all should've seen the look on his face when I told him how much Santi was paying me!" Primetime continued. "He was sick."

"Primetime...you are interrupting my lesson," Santi interrupted. He was visibly upset, but remained calm. Don't listen to liars and deceivers...or idiots. Give yourself a chance. Allow your money to grow. Invest wisely. You'll succeed if you take opportunity, rather than wait for it."

"Hey kid," said Primetime, sliding the cocaine-laden plate my way. "How old are you?"

"25," I replied, wondering what Primetime was about to speak on. "Do you have ADHD? You need Adderall."

It was a true test to pay attention to Santiago's lesson while listening to a drunk Irishman talk about criminal endeavors of his past. How did I get here, to this twilight zone?

"Oh ok well shit yeah, I was about your age now. I was in Kentucky at the time. I had gotten a phone call one day on 20 pounds up in Cincinnati. The motherfucker only wanted 35 grand for 'em but me and my girl were supposed to have dinner that night. It was nothing that couldn't wait until the next day, but fuck it, I was trying to be nice," Primetime shrugged his shoulders. "Ya know, special and shit."

"And she still left your shitty ass," Robbie jeered. "Hey kid if you're not going to do the blow, pass it."

Everyone eyed me as I scooped a butter knife full of powder onto my own plate and slid the mountainous porcelain to Robbie. Geronimo asked if I were a resourceful piece of shit but I didn't answer, separating my hoard into lines as Primetime continued his story.

"Fuck you Robbie. Anyway kid, I go up there the next day and my guy only has ten pounds left, so I drive back home with 10 bows in my truck bed and 17 grand sitting on my backseat. I was so upset about missing out on all twenty that I rolled a blunt for the road. Needless to say, my ass got pulled over going 72 in a 70 mile per hour zone. Luckily, they only took my money."

"What about the weed?" I asked, looking up at Primetime while tooting a line.

"Didn't even call for dogs."

My eyebrows lowered as I sat, perplexed. "So you got a civil forfeiture citation and came home with the weed?"

"Pretty much," Robbie shrugged.

"That's 'cause he's white," muffled Robbie while striking a match to light the cigar hanging in his mouth. "Troopers would have torn any of our cars apart over that shit."

"That may very well be true, but that isn't the lesson in this. My guy ended up selling ten to a guy for forty fucking grands. I couldn't be upset at him though," Primetime leaned back in his chair, took a deep breath and sipped his glass. "The lesson is to take full advantage of opportunity and not be distracted by desires and romantic canoodling. The only person standing in your way is you."

"Canoodling? The fuck is that? Plus, it sounds like if the only person standing in your way was you, then you should've moved,"

Shelby crowed.

We each erupted into laughter at Shelby's random outburst. His point was extreme, and very true. Maybe Primetime should have gotten out of his own way. The statement 'You are the only one standing in your way' is extremely near-sighted, blatantly false and basically true only in the most trivial sense. Imbecilic in every sense of the entirety of the word.

"Man, you know what the fuck I mean," Primetime retorted. Wining and dining bitches."

"And that's probably the reason she left your ass. Hell, you could have taken her on the ride, gotten a hotel and stopped at a restaurant the next day or some shit," Shelby chastised, diming the lightness of the conversation. "That's simple shit really."

"Kid, shut the fuck up." Primetime leaned into the table, looking towards Shelby with a menacing glare. Shelby smirked and made himself a line.

"What the fuck is funny?" asked Primetime.

Shelby took a bump of coke to his nose and snorted before speaking. "How do you all feel about feminism?"

Each of us looked to each other in hopes of receiving some sort of clarification on what in the flying fuck my brother was talking about. I looked to Corey and he returned the same expression; our minced faces mirrored one another's. What has the plight of a man on the verge of signing his soul over to a woman done to my brother? Feminism?

"Man, what?" Geronimo asked. I was surprised to see that he was confused as Corey and I.

"Well," Shelby began, making himself another line of coke. "Here's how I feel. Sherman, say that you and Primetime work at a factory together. You all do the same type of work, however there are quite a number of unknown variables. Variable one…" Shelby says, looking at Primetime. "He is a woman. That is very homely and mannish. Sherman is himself. A scrawny little shit of a man."

"Bitch, you look like your neck blew a bubble," Primetime joked.

"OOOH," said Shelby sarcastically. "Great joke. Anyway. Sherm, you're made to lift and sort 80 pound boxes each day while the six foot, one hundred and eighty-seven-pound female Primetime tosses around ten and fifteen pound boxes. Sherm, you should get paid more right?"

"Hell yeah. Fuck Primetime. That She or he or who the fuck ever should be lifting heavy shit."

"It's not my fault that I was built like a linebacker. What's your point kid?" Primetime asked.

"I was just changing the subject," Shelby replied.

Robbie hadn't said much, and I found it peculiar. He had spoken only a few words. I suppose running his index finger around the lip of his glass while listening to the table converse was more important. His face was sordid as he listened to our conversation, a complete contrast from the smile that he beamed upon our introduction. This smile, the one that put me at ease and made me feel that everything would be alright even though I was eating dinner with murderous villains, was replaced by a glare of repugnancy.

"Robbie, what's pulling your dick?" I asked.

He didn't answer my question, choosing to wipe his teeth with his tongue flashing that revolting gaze at me.

"Pay your taxes, kid," said Robbie.

"Have you ever paid taxes?" I asked. "Cause from the looks of it…"

"If you can dodge bullets you can dodge an IRS audit," Robbie replied.

"So why are you asking me if I pay my taxes?" I asked.

"Well, with what we're about to give you…" Robbie let out a long sigh before continuing. "Nothing is difficult and anything that you wish to accomplish will be easily had. With that said, hard work & sacrifice do not build wealth. They build resentment, but they do not build wealth. The plane that we are on…everything is easy. Anything that is difficult is not meant."

"Basically what the fucker is saying is that we need a percentage" Primetime ejaculated. "Robbie likes to talk in circles."

I didn't bother responding to their statement. Percentage? A percentage from what? What did these men, this group called Heaven, expect me to do? I became irritated and confused; upset that I had no idea what plans Heaven had for me. My forehead began to sweat and nausea came over me.

I wanted to rise from my chair but my body refused to listen to my brain and its plea to rise and exit. I had no time to do so anyway however…Santi's other guests had arrived.

Santi rose from his seat and walked to Pedro, who was

speaking with two men at the entrance. Pedro began searching one of the men but Santi told him that it was unnecessary. I'm not sure what else was said during their entrance, however Santi returned to the table visibly angry. His eyes were bloodshot red. With his temples and jaws pulsating and fist clenched, I wondered what type of exchange he and the men had. The men followed Santi to the table that we sat, however none of us nor Santi or his security asked them if they wanted to be seated. They didn't ask either as they stood behind Shelby, Corey and I motionless. It is an eerie feeling to be surrounded with men that want to give you something. In this day and age, nothing is free and everything can get you killed.

"Sherman."

I felt a large hand grasp my shoulder. The touch sent a chill down my spine and for the first time since landing in Las Vegas I felt terror.

"I have a proposition. Please don't disappoint us."

I didn't budge, however the stares that I felt coming from Heaven and my comrades changed my fear into anger. Who in the hell did this douche think he was? Both of them for that matter. Only one had spoken so far, the other stood with a pen and paper. We were all unsure of exactly what they wanted.

"Who in the fuck are you?" I rang. I shrugged my shoulder violently and with cocaine visible on the tip of my nose, I turned to face both men while grabbing my glass of bourbon. I was tempted to throw it. Both men wore white suits which I thought was extremely odd for Las Vegas...hell, anywhere for that matter. Who in the fuck would wear a white suit, knowing that you have the chance to get anything from stripper cum to chocolate all over it? I turned back around and gave Santi a look of quandary. He must have heard my silent imploration.

"Hell no. I don't know who in the fuck these ass clowns are. Pedro, bring these fucks another table. They wanna be assholes, we'll treat these assholes like segregation is legal."

I don't think that any of us would have reacted to him if we were sober. We all would have sat there and ate crumpets and drank tea like the civilized individuals we were. Yes, the table at which we sat would display nothing but the positive influence that each of us created, held, and dispensed at will. If only that were the case...however it was far from it. We were savages. Disgusting, vile, terrible savage's hell bent on committing sins that these mice could not fathom. And we would not apologize. We should not and will not apologize for who we are. Especially since the one in front of us has made us this way.

"Santi! You motherfucker," Primetime yelled. "Turn down your awesome alright. These assholes can't be thinking straight. That's no way to introduce yourself to prospective business partners. And it's fucking up my cognition. I'm not rational."

"Partners? Who said anything about being partners? We own."

I couldn't tell which of the men in the white suits spoke. Own? Who, me? They mustn't know how to treat people. In this world that we live in, we've all got a reason to treat one another better. It's our duty to be the nicest that we can be to everyone. Don't be an asshole. But fuck that in this situation. These two assholes, dressed in their white clown suits with wing-tip shoes, blonde hair peeking from underneath the top-hats that sat on the crowns of their heads, had come to me to offer a job. A job so lucrative and influential that I'd have to already be worth ten figures to decline the invitation into the position.

I was apprehensive about going over to their table. Afraid, in a 'wow, this may not end very well' type of way...hell, when's the last time you were set up and placed in a situation? A situation that you thought you had the power to control, that you thought you chose to place yourself in? This situation was foreign. I felt nothing but worry, a jittery coked out worry.

~

My moist palms gripped the handles of my chair as I moved backwards, standing to walk to the ass clowns table. They sat, smug and important looking. One wore a blue tie, the other a red one. The red tie sat to my right, blue to the left. What is it with this uniformity...it is quite odd, that this town, this place that I love and have begun to hate, is as irregular as it is. What do these men want? Why have they sought me? And why in the flying fuck did Santi go along with this mess?

I must have tooted an eight ball in the thirty minutes that Heaven, Corey, Shelby and I sat talking...and I have absolutely no idea what in the fuck is going on. I'm lost, obviously out of my league. How did I manage to get myself into this situation, I thought that I had done everything right...?

Walking over to them proved difficult as the anger that I felt morphed back into fear. I felt it creep from the restaurant floor up my legs like vines, my body struggling more and more as I uprooted them with each reluctant step. I was cautious as a cat, eying them for several seconds prior to sitting. Their dark eyes and crooked smiles, these men stared me down as wolves do sheep. Each time they spoke, I saw only sharp teeth and saliva, their voices roaring blasphemy as I had never heard before.

"Sherman, we want you to write. But you'd have to do it our way. You'll win prestigious awards, make millions of dollars and influence millions upon millions of people ten times over, all over the world," The creepy bastard to the left spoke.

The jerk to the right looked me up and down. He sat, writing things in a note pad, jotting. I wondered what in the fuck he was writing as I sat across from them, their beady eyes piercing into me as they attempted to peer into my soul.

People like these two are terrible entities. They aren't human. They are devilish creatures that roam the lands for souls to entrap, and they wished for me to be one. I looked back towards Heaven; they sat with a dark cloud over their heads watching me intently.

"We'd like to take the art of writing in a new direction in America. You're a rap fan, right? Sure you are. Well, the same thing that happened to them, we want to do to writing."

What happened to them? Who was them? Rap artists? The rap genre itself? Rap music has become as ignorant as any other thing in the world, and just as popular. Rightfully so too. It is a culture. Yet, it has been utilized by numerous people in power to keep a profitable industry thriving. Disgusting indeed, as an entire society has undergone severe brainwashing and psychotherapy, so much so that the action of harming one another is nothing but a reflex. Perpetuating crime in music had been a ploy created by music industry executives and assholes in high profile positions in the private prison industry. This ploy was one that would enhance the evident detriment to minorities.

"The music industry has invested money into privately built prisons for years. Over 25 to be exact. We want to make your writings...we want to take them and use your influence as well as ours, to impact the profitability of these investments. Numerous publishing houses have invested into these prisons. How does it sound?"

This fucker really asked me how it sounds. This is insane and down-right frightful. How did I get into this situation? I didn't ask for this shit, fuck this. I gazed in amazement, mouth open wide as the man to the left continued his sales pitch.

"The more motherfuckers we get in these prisons, the more the government pays. We've got it down to a science. We even buy stocks. It's fucking incredible," the bastard iterated slyly, his voice low and smooth.

"What?" I asked, my mouth opened. "You want me to write about criminal shit so I send more black people to jail?"

"Yes, in a nutshell."

"Is this a fucking joke!"

Suddenly the man to the right, the one that had been looking me up and down, jotting notes as if he were a stenographer in court, pulled a small revolver from his waist band and set it on the table.

I glared at the man, wondering what the best possible scenario of this situation could be. I didn't want to cause a ruckus and I surely did not want to be sitting at this table with two lunatics.

What in the world is happening? I've got to be dreaming, asleep...that's it. That's got to be reality. Why in the fuck does it have to be my day? How does this type of bullshit happen? Twice in one hour? God damn it and whoever loves it to hell!

"It would be in your best interest to agree."

I leaned into my chair, dazed and confused. I wondered what the outcome of the night, hell, this meeting, would be. I understood the enormity of this situation and it made me feel as small as a grain of sand in a 100-gallon aquarium. My nerves were shot. A crude sense of desperation welled over me. Run. Run fast and far. You're jacked up on cocaine Sherman, a ridiculous amount of it. I'm sure you could make it to Mandalay Bay, as long as pedestrian ped-way traffic is minimal.

The weekend cocaine binge that I was on was doing a number on me. I had become reacquainted with the devil and become a godless heathen. This substance, the wretched and vile creator of mania that halts the catalyst that begets suffering from hate. The substance that makes borne from hate, anger and from that, fear. Fuck fear. Cocaine was my savior for the moment and with it coursing through my body I transmuted into a being more than human. I am the god with the goods and everything in the world be damned, conquer I shall. The cocaine had made me more aware of the situation and everything that surrounded me.

I looked around and witnessed the waiter gallop speedily to pour bourbon into the seven challis' standing royally at my friends table, and I began to hone in on the music that was being played in the background.

The music, the voice…it sounded distant, yet I was able to feel the sounds as if they were being blasted in a vehicle that I was merrily cruising in. No longer was the voice of an imposter Biggie Pritchard coming from the speakers throughout the front of the restaurant. No, it was an angelic voice, one that comforted your inner being with a sweet serenade and attracted you to it as a magnet would its opposite. A voice that was syrupy and soothing, a nectar that pleasantly over-powered the bitter state of affairs that enclosed me at the present moment. I could not see with my own eyes the woman whose voice was rippling through the air, affecting me in the same way that the sun and the water affect the plumage of a rain forest. Seductive and lovely, it drew me in with such vigor that I was forced to rise from the table and get a visual of the Siren and her beauteous melody.

"Where are you going? We're in the middle of something!" was faintly heard by my ears, yet I was so enamored by the peace that I was receiving from the sounds vibrating through the air that I paid whoever spoke no mind. Exiting the back dining area in which we politicized, I gasped, dropping my Challis', particles of glass strewing everywhere. My leather dress shoes had taken the brunt of the wave of liquor that escaped the challis but that was no matter. Several people turned in their chairs upon the smashing of my crockery, yet I felt that they were miniscule specks of sand in a universe that had immensely grown in the past three minutes. Fuck them. The voice that I was hearing was not one that I knew, yet it sounded eerily familiar.

As I stood outside of the doorway of the backroom dining area of the restaurant, the stage directly in front of me and rows of tables positioned throughout, I did the only thing that I felt I could do. There was no more time to think, hell, I had neither the want nor the ability to...my brain may very well have short-circuited if I even tried. My body began a slow strut down the middle of an aisle that resembled the passage way of the Israelite's during their gallivanted march through the Red Sea.

I made an undeviating straight line towards the alluring vocalization of the woman on stage, giving no care to any other patron inside. From afar I gazed at a single light shone from the rafters on an illustrious indigo sequined dress contouring this woman with the angelic voice. Could it be? Had I found her again at last? Had she come back to haunt me once more? Heaven cannot be far; I am sure of it. I walked down the aisle, approaching slowly as a lion would a gazelle in African grassland. She seemed so far away.

My heart beat rapidly as my breathing increased and, a slight fear came over me as I wondered if I could die from a welling of emotion inside of the heart. I thought that I would never see her again. The closer I got to her, the more wondrous a feeling that I had never once in life felt gained control of me. It was glorious and orgasmic, and seeing this woman standing in front of me so elegantly and unattached made this feeling escape through my pores.

Her blonde hair placed in a style reminiscent of the 1950's up-do, with rolled bangs and full lips of beguiling red lipstick, I was utterly astonished by the glory that I saw. Standing at the base of the stage, the crowd to the rear of me and a miracle staring down at me, I watched and listened as Melody sang an opus of love to me so sincere and pure that a virgin would taint it. Her light shone onto me and mine onto her and we stared into one another's eyes.

I came to the senile realization that I was in fact, in love. A real love, a perfect love. Not a love as one would a scar, growing to love a damage or an imperfection. No, this was real. A love of pure matter and one of no attachment.

Interlude

Love is a crazy thing. Well, romantic love. Love between a man and a woman, that kind of love. It's odd because you can totally love multiple people at one time or love the wrong person. What kind of love is that? Is that some real shit or just a figment of the imagination with feelings involved? It just seems so ridiculous to me. What on fucking earth would possess a person to love the wrong person? Timing? A lot of those love gurus say that timing is everything in love connections, and I say fuck them. This whole soul mate thing, what in the flying fuck is a soul mate? How in the fuck do you know if you have a soul mate? Say that shit out loud and listen to just how stupid you sound. It feels good to know that your soul mate is having sex with other people, doesn't it?

Just because you and another person think about each other at the same time, sending "hey" texts and shit like that. Just because you and that same person can go without speaking for months on end and upon seeing one another, fall right back in love. Just because everything about your relationship is terrible and horrendous things have been done to one another, yet much is looked over due to the connection that you two share...does not fucking mean that you are soul mates.

Have you ever sat and thought about how stupid your ass has to be to stay with a person that blatantly disrespects you and their own self, as well as you blatantly disrespecting them and your own self? It's pointless. Why? Because you're fucking crazy, that's why. Einstein said lose your attachments, Jesus said lose your attachments, Buddha and Lao Tzu said the same fucking thing as well.

I will tell you by God, women will drive you insane, and the right one will make you never want to have a romantic relationship ever again. The woman will rip out a piece of your soul and play with it while you writhe in pain. Hopefully it happens at a young age and not in your 30's or 40's, because you might as well kill yourself, or dabble in drugs. It'll make life more enjoyable, knowing that your wife was cheating on you and your child may not be yours.

Going through my first heartbreak at the ripe old age of 24, hard drug use became a necessity. MDMA was the first serious drug that I tried. Even though I've been smoking marijuana since 13, I had never ventured into any type of drug besides prescription pills…which I now despise. Seeing someone get hit in the head with a hammer and not remember because he was too loaded on bars will cause that to happen. I was always a wussy when it came to those things anyway.

At 18, I was good with a tab ten and a beer. Fast forward 6 years, a girlfriend that cheated on me, a baby mama that started as a side chick, and another side chick that I fell in love with, I was due for some ignorance.

As a guy, it sucks when your girl gives her attention to someone else. It sucks even more when the person is familiar with her or her family. What's worse is when the motherfucker is familiar with you. Even worse is when you are familiar with the other person. And the worst part is when it's multiple motherfuckers that are familiar with you and you with them. Shocker: most females want to do hoe shit. They insist on having sex with multiple men, sometimes in the same day. Ok, Ok, you can say that men engage in this type of behavior all of the time and there is nothing wrong with it. Liberate women, blah blah blah.

Ladies, I am here to tell you that there are no double standards. There is a standard for men and a standard for women. The standard for men is to treat women with respect. You don't have to share your passion and energy with any and every one.

The same goes for women. Although sex is fun as hell and not at all bad, becoming the monk that I have become I cannot bring myself to share shit. I have super powers and will change your fucking life and by God, this shit is sacred and amazing. I'm not just anybody. You can't be a whole, filling up a half. It must be two wholes together, so the energies are not depleted. This will also equate to a true romantic love, which brings me to Alexia. As you can probably tell, I've been talking about her monkey ass. She called.

SATURDAY, 8 P.M. PST

You know, there are always mishaps that go on in your life. One minute you're riding the wave of forever-ness into the sunset and then boom, an asteroid comes and knocks you off of your inter-galactic rainbow. Linking with Alexia was the asteroid that fucked up my entire balance. Lord have mercy, why do I allow the woman to have utter control over my emotions, knowing that she is an irresponsible and irreconcilably evil person, intent on destroying every ounce of manhood that I possess.

What you see is what you get.

I saw her as much more than a demonic Lilith. She was a sweet candy, a ray of sun that I was attached to in such a way that I identified myself and my worth as her. She was a work of art; a disturbingly beautiful epistolary essay, a frightening and delicate sculpture, a painting as abstract as ocean waves. I hold the assumption that these types of people; those that are splendidly complex, easy to look at yet difficult to comprehend, attractive yet more superb because of the grim non-understanding associated with their character and personality, should be embraced and studied. At least once in your life, you should fall in love with a beautiful lie. I attempted to understand everything about this creature, this human that wanted so much to be tamed yet dared one to corral her.

I was set to meet her at Smith in 30 minutes, a rendezvous point of sorts. Our first date 5 years ago commenced at a hibachi restaurant, Smith, in Cincinnati, Ohio.

She had been jubilant in her expression of distaste for Chinese food when we chatted through text messages about our meeting, which baffled me because we had exchanged numbers at a Chinese fast food restaurant. Both of her hands carried white plastic bags filled to the brim with take-out and I even helped her carry an extra bag that she held between her teeth. Jokes about her food carrying methods turned into small talk about the weather and her having never been on the Big Four walking bridge located in downtown Louisville. An exchange of phone numbers led to dinner and a hike up an incline and across a bridge over the Ohio River.

On our slow walk across the bridge, a light breeze blew in 78-degree weather as the stars sparkling in the night sky reflected elegantly off of the dark water. I felt more different than I ever had before, standing with her, looking west towards the moon and the downtown of Louisville.

Seeing that downtown Louisville is really uptown and the earth's rotation makes the moon appear to rise in the east and set in the west, I should have been aware of the enormity of this occasion; an illusion that I believed. Oh, what a night, if only Joshua would halt the movement of rocks in orbit, I'd be able to be still and aware to the fact that everything is indeed moving the opposite of what I see.

Yet, this feeling that I gained...I embraced it, I wanted it to continue. Like a crack head searching for that initial high, I became attached to something that was no good for me; something that I should have detached from and let go... the feeling that welled and rose inside of me. This is the danger of desiring an emotion or a feeling; they are designed to be fleeting, to not be around for long.

Entering the restaurant, I approached the host with a raised right hand, holding two fingers in the air.

"Randolph?" the host asked. As I nodded my head she bent down behind her podium and rose with two menus. "How are you doing today Mr. Randolph? Right this way."

I was 30 minutes premature, but had called earlier in the day that I would be arriving at this time. Having Santiago place my reservation had a lot to do with the preferential treatment that I was set to receive. The star role is mine in this movie however.

I was led to a room in the very back of the restaurant. This room held a hibachi grill and a personal chef. A bright smile and a head nod from the chef greeted me as I sat. I returned the same greeting as the waitress placed menus in front and to the right of me. Turning toward her, I asked "May I order a large house Saki please? Warm. Thank you."

A smile and a head nod is the only answer that I was afforded as she scurried off. I turned back around to face the chef, who had begun to sharpen his knife. His vigorous back and forth strokes between the knife and sharpener grabbed my attention so tightly that I would have become hypnotized if not for the chef opening his mouth and introducing himself...

"My name is Jeffrey,"

I adjusted my vision to observe this chef, a person that looked to be of Japanese descent working as a hibachi grill extraordinaire in a Japanese restaurant, whose name just so happened to be Jeffrey. My eyes squinted and my forehead wrinkled in sheer astonishment as I sat there and wondered why this chef's name was Jeffrey. I suppose I shouldn't be too dumbfounded, but people don't get to be amazed in this type of way very often.

"Is that your real name?" I couldn't help it. I had too. It's a valid question. Luckily he smiled and set the kitchenware onto his cart. I'm just glad that he decided not to chop me in half with his miniature samurai sword.

"Yes, my name is Jeffrey, man. I'm from motherfucking Compton homie."

I sat back, confused and amazed at the enormity of what I just heard. Did this Asian man just say he was from Compton? Intrigued by the uniqueness of the man, I began to question him.

"You're from Compton? How often does that shit happen?" I asked.

"A lot homie. It's 2016 cuz, it's different type niggas everywhere."

"Are you in a gang?" ...I sounded like a pre-teen suburban white girl asking her first middle school black boyfriend if he's ever been to the hood before.

"YEAH HOMIE!"

I rose from my seat, startled to high hell by two things. One being the chef's escalation of voice and the second, a loud crash coming from behind me that sounded as if a small bomb had been detonated. These people are crazy...I bet Santi had hired them to murder me and hide me in a freezer. Hell, they may even use my body parts as food for their guests. The filet mignon strips that made your mouth water while the hibachi all-star sliced and diced and grilled them with the flare of a circus? Do you remember those? It was a special order made by your cousin specifically for you; never having eaten at a hibachi restaurant as if you were a third-world citizen, your cousin wanted you to ingest the finest meat that this restaurant had to offer.

Becoming one of the more successful event promoters in Las Vegas came with a price for your cousin and, he had managed to make several enemies. Yet and still, he insisted on comp'ing you for a weekend in Vegas for your birthday. Oh yes, yes Lord. Have mercy on your soul. You shall enjoy the finest that Heaven has to offer...after all, Heaven IS in Las Vegas. Everything that your heart desires will be afforded to you, because hell, everyone loves sex and everyone loves serotonin and dopamine and everyone wants to experience the greatness inside. Indeed, you were due for a grand trip. Shame how even with everything you want in your reach, you still manage to get fucked. Those strips you devoured and expressed so much love and gratefulness for? My adductor muscles...Apparently your cousin had fucked up on a favor for Mr. Mora and good old Santi wanted him to taste his demise. Unfortunately, a favor toward you from your cousin resulted in repulsiveness directly involving you. Sometimes, things not meant for you end up in your possession. Watch who you associate with, they may be guiding disaster directly towards you.

Snapping out of my day-dream, I turned around and saw the host staring at the broken ceramic kettle, two ceramic shot glasses and wooden board at her feet. The look on her face was of utter repugnance and as she lifted her head, chills ran down my spine. She was possessed. I was tempted to throw something at her...a knife would be the most reasonable weapon...and that's when she walked into the room, and the chaos that was in progress ceased to go on, or in my vision at the very least, it ceased to exist.

All five feet five inches of evenly toned skin the color of a peeled banana. A scarlet dress covered her body from her shoulder to three inches above the top of her knee cap. The dress wrapped tightly around her body in the same fashion that the skin on an apple wraps around the meat of the fruit, or a race car wraps around a curve on a lonely highway in Southern California.

I recognized the dress instantly, the neck line of it plunging below her supple collarbone, a feature that I noticed on the dress while purchasing it in Los Angeles in 2012 while on a business trip.

Los Angeles was a decent time, as I smoked enough marijuana to make my feet fall off and lungs turn to charcoal. The atmosphere on Venice Beach was amazing. Young white men danced and solicited medical marijuana cards while a celebrity basketball game commenced. Curly haired women roller-bladed and teens with dyed hair and cut-off jeans scrambled around as five year olds do on the elementary school playground. It was utterly glorious and free, people smoking pot as if it were the 1960's.

Everyone seemingly is surrounded by nature or with nature, especially since a natural creation is so loved and cherished. Water, sky, land…Venice Beach has it all. It is incredible to be able to take off your shoes and place your feet into the wet sand, feeling the earth from your roots. The sand casting your feet like you broke that motherfucker in a freak accident with a bowling ball…

Sidenote: Never drop a bowling ball on a toe, especially if you're a dumb ass ten-year-old hell bent on seeing how high you can thrust a 16-pound marble sporting instrument into the air. Kids are fucking ridiculous.

…It is lovely to be able to saunter onto a cluster of rocks jutting into the ocean from the beach, hopping from one to the next until you realize that 100 feet away is your only hope of survival, and if the wind decides to gust, bringing an incredible tidal wave of ocean water, you will surely be knocked back into your mother's womb. You'll be able to notice the palm trees and how the leaves sway with the wind. Yes, you will notice the palm trees and you must also notice the man seated directly underneath one, selling oranges.

Do not approach this man. DO NOT approach any man sitting underneath a tree selling delectable fruit.

I purchased an orange before, and the one time I dared too, I found that it was the most delicious orange that I had ever tasted. So delicious that I was forced to kick the poor man in his legs repeatedly, so much so that he had a hard time getting up. Seeing him having such a hard time and knowing that it was his orange that caused the rage in my heart to overflow because it was so damned good, I took his entire burlap sack of them. Those oranges are extremely dangerous and are what I attribute my temporary insanity too. However, I had taken 3 bars and drank a pint of bourbon prior to the leg beating of this man who only wanted to sell oranges. And I am not ashamed.

I always suspected that the palm trees had some crazy freak hypnotizing mind power over people, the power to destroy everything that makes humans inherently human. I bet the Buddha sat under a palm tree, all happy and absorbent, not giving a flying fuck about a damn thing, except for rising to the sun. Buddha, you sly devil…

Los Angeles, such a beauty. I had ventured there with friends from high school. We had kept in contact for years, real friends. A naval officer stationed in San Diego and a flight attendant working for a major airline accompanied me on my trip, which began and ended in San Diego. One night in San Diego, the initial night, ended in such terror that it had no choice but to lead into the next day. I almost had a mental breakdown. Arriving in the magnificent city, a few miles away from Mexico, I was excited.

Daniel, a great buddy of mine whom I admired for his approach to life, picked Sasha and I up from the airport and drove us towards his home, which he said was located directly across the expressway. I thought to myself that a pretty dope weekend was going to begin, but lord have mercy...I had no idea what in the fuck I was in for. After placing our luggage into his home, Daniel directed us towards a door in his kitchen leading to his basement. His wooden steps creaked and you could smell the odor of damp concrete leading to the unfinished basement emanating from the pores of its walls. Step by step we addled down this steep and noisy staircase until we reached a lightly carpeted floor. A flick of a light switch on a wall by Daniel brightened the space revealing a room full of so much booze that I was stricken with alcohol poisoning by simply being there. 1000 varied bottles of assorted brands of alcohol and champagne sat on the floor in a mass rivaling any tumor seen on TV.

That night began with us drinking vodka and premium beer, continued with the consumption of gold tequila, and ended with a ride through downtown San Diego on a carriage being cycled around by a teenaged white kid. The horror was the scene of a black military man and an Asian woman heaving their intestines into toilets; the shrieks and moans coming from the bathrooms causing the entire house to rumble.

The sound of the human body rejecting the liquid poison that it had earlier ingested is one that even a witch would despise. Wailing and moaning as banshees or dying seals and sea lions do, Daniel and Sasha writhed in pain as their intestinal systems worked over time to rid their bodies of fermented venom, as I sat on the couch, laughing hysterically at those poo putt drinkers. Trepidation would come in the morning for me however, as I awoke at 7 a.m. to a belly knotted in such a way that the only thing I could do was crawl and sigh. Death came for me quickly that morning and afternoon, as I was not fit to travel to LA until 3 p.m.

I was a total mess; a wreck of a man. There I lay on the cold linoleum of Daniels first floor bathroom, shirt off and curled into the fetal position. I barely moved that morning and afternoon, save for the mustering of an amount of strength so minute that even pulling myself up by the toilet in order to hurl a thick yellow liquid that tasted of death into the toilet bowl left me exhausted.

This one night in San Diego: I died; yet I keep with me lovely memories of politicking with marijuana growers over cups of tea while sitting on La Jolla Shores. I remember as if I were there: Seals and Sea Lions lie on a large rock that juts upward out of the ocean, as a large pimple on persons' nose would. Men deep sea fish and couples stroll around, hands clasped tightly, allowing the wind to carry their love and fill the area. Pleasant and pleasing it is to inhale love and joy, abundance and prosperity; and exhale stress and doubt, fear and worry.

I hold the belief that the collarbone on a woman is the most beautiful thing that God equipped women with. Showing ever so gracefully in low rising blouses and even more so in bras or in the nude, the female collarbone has the ability to drive a man insane. So sensitive, so delicate…a short punch to it could break the motherfucker in two…however, the striking appearance of it is something that one is so enamored with that I dare not. Slight kisses, simple pecks and caresses should be the only action delivered to the ever so divine bone that is called clavicle.

A small gold necklace hung from Alexia's neck, the charm molded into two gold hearts interlocked, forming an unbreakable connection. Her long legs seemed to stretch for miles from her feet, which were being held hostage by black high heels. A gorgeous site to behold, yes she was. The joy and pain that I felt during our love and after our end came rushing back. Had I made the correct decision by meeting her? Damn it, what in the hell was I thinking? She has no interest in anything associated with you or even you yourself, so damn it Sherman, why in the flying hell would you put yourself in this situation? She did leave you for Christ sake.

Hell, I'm right. I have a prerogative not to be in this place, sitting in front of man from Compton while the person that owns my heart waltz's up and orders Filet Mignon, Lobster and Shrimp on my tab. Fuck that shit!...

But, I'm already here.

My mind had been made to attend this emotional debacle,

weeks in advance. I was prepared.

Watching her strut to the table, I felt the urge to snort a line of cocaine so long that a motherfucker would think it was a tape worm. I was nervous, so very nervous. How would she react to this? She can handle me angry, tired, crazed, delirious, and even depressed...but nervous? She'd never seen such. It would be something that she would not understand...The waitress better hurry back with those sake shots. I have no desire to tip her for staring at my date for the night...she must work!

As Alexia approached, I rose from my seat to step around and pull hers out. A smile ran across her face, large and warming.

"My dress," I muttered, and as she blushed I smiled back, pushing her chair forward. I returned to my seat and noticed my nervousness had fled. I was not devoid however. The feeling had been replaced with something that I had felt before, a long time ago. The test that I did not pass years ago in a restaurant similar to this was upon me, yet I had learned my lesson and was ready to show it this time around.

Yes, I will enjoy this feeling, I will enjoy this moment. Present. I will be present in this moment. I will not hold to this moment, I will not seek this moment, this emotion, this feeling.

"How are you?" Her voice was calm and soothing, angelic to the man who rid himself of demons once he rid himself of her. But, you never really rid yourself of demons...they go on to others once you gain power over them, the power to quell them and make them seem infantile and under control. Most people's demons come from other people...Do not feed the wolves, the egos, of these people. Their demons may get you....So I will be aware and mindful. Do not feed her ego.

"I'm good. You're wonderful."

FUCK! As is innate in every human experience...when you tell yourself what you aren't going to do, you shall be presented with an opportunity to prove it. Damn it....Oh well, fuck it.

"Thank you," she replied.

A silence fell over us for a few seconds as I stared into space while she looked me up and down. It felt like an eternity.

I smelled her. All of her...her perfume was sweet and unfamiliar. It made me inhale deeply, the fragrance filling my chest with its honeyed scent of nectar. Her scent was almost unbearable. It was driving me crazy. I wondered what she thought of me after the past five months. She was beautiful as ever and even more intriguing due to the fact that she confused the flying fuck out of me. I was baffled that she only responded with a "thank you". This isn't the Alexia I know. Oh hell no, the Alexia I know would harp on and on about her hair or clothes or handbag or shoes, the reasons why she was "wonderful". Maybe, I thought, she had learned to control her own ego and appreciate small comments of warmth and creep-ness.

INTERLUDE II

Losing and creating myself, discovering a long buried passion, feels as a man would who returns from war that has not seen his wife and children in five years' time. I was once an agonized soul, tortured by my own way of thinking, crippled not only by my thought process but also my thoughts. Controlling reaction, learning not to react...I formed into this person that truly believed that he could be an amazing writer. Can I actually change the way of a man's thinking by allowing him to read my quirky tales of adventure in Las Vegas? This will surely push the limit of ones...anyone's, consciousness. I suppose that eventually, will have to analyze the legitimate dichotomy of a real person living the rock star life while also living, loving; being a family man. My mother often used the term 'hippie' to describe me...this may be true, however I am not always a peace loving individual and I'll be damned if I hug a tree or give a damn about a stupid ass furry rabbit that would be a wonderful meat in a vegetable stew. Chaos is wonderful and I feed off of it...Who in the fuck are you in my world anyway? My life is my life. I see with my own eyes and am aware of my own moments. What you view is not what I view. What you feel is not what I feel. I am rare. And I live this way. Maybe Alexia has finally caught on to what I have been trying to tell her.

SATURDAY, 8:49 P.M PST

"Do I have to be all formal with you two niggas? You already know where I'm from and shit homie," The chef said, cutting my daydream short.

Fuck it, everybody get comfortable.

"Yeah fam, you're cool. You scared the shit out of the little waitress lady," I replied.

"Her fault. She always getting startled and shit, bugging out looking like a fucking clucker."

I wanted to laugh at the gangster ass chef but I refrained. His accent was authentic. He really had to be a Compton baby. This has got to be the dopest shit on earth...it's not very often you get a private table at Smith with a personal chef from Compton.

Alexia sat smiling at me, her hazel eyes shining in the overhead lights. She had dyed her hair to a dark brown, a tone that I found to make her features stand out. Fat cheeks, a large forehead and voluptuous lips covered in red lipstick, I was entranced by her. Either I am implausibly brilliant or really fucking stupid for this meeting...only time will tell.

"How have you been?" Alexia's voice entered my ears and reverberated in my head as a drum quartet's melody bouncing off of the walls of an atrium would.

"I've been wonderful. No complaints. How is LA treating you?" I replied.

"It's great, I love Venice. I'm in Hollywood a lot, ya know, directing, but my little quiet place is my joy."

I squinted my eyes at Alexia, rearing my head back in a struck manner...directing?

"Why you looking like that?" She asked, confused.

"You direct? What happened to you doing the fucking thing?"

"I never was going to do that," She said mockingly.

"What? You told me that you were," I could feel sweat beginning to form on my brow.

"Porn? Y'all some freaky bitches fasho. Look, I'm about to go holler at the piss pot. Be right back," the chef interjected.

I looked Alexia up and down, admiring her beauty while also

tangled as to how in the fuck I could have possibly missed that she was directing instead of performing.

"No. I told you I was moving to LA and would be doing some things in the porn business. It was a tentative offer, so I didn't want to be definite to what I would be doing. If it had anything to do with having sex, I wouldn't have gone."

"But you broke up with me dog."

"No, dog. My nigga," Alexia said with a beautiful and southern twang. She was a woman that could stop a shootout or tell a doctor precisely what was wrong with a patient. "You got all fucked up and mad when I told you. You weren't hearing shit. You told me to get the fuck out."

"But Goddamn, you weren't really supposed to leave!"

"What in the flying fuck do you expect nigga!" Alexia said as she shoved me in my right shoulder. This young woman can push with some force, damn it to hell. I'd been the recipient of several punches to the chin from her, even a wooden broom that was snapped in two over my head. She seemed stronger however. The gangster chef had strolled off to the restroom leaving us here to do one of two things; bicker or make love. Right now we were on the former however the latter was not far off. Get us together, alone, and I guarantee there will be sexual fireworks.

Grabbing my face with her hands, she pulled me closer and looked deeply into my eyes...

"Look, I'm sorry I broke up with you," Alexia began.

Shivers went down my spine as I let out an extraneous sigh. The sensual touch of a woman is something that a man cannot resist.

It is odd, this relationship that Alexia and I have held. It is the mystery. Both men and women love to be fascinated by the mystery in the person that they see themselves with, and Alexia loved to remain a mystery, and also a misery, to me. A little mystery in your romance can go a long way and Alexia relished the clandestine and enigmatic unknowing in our passion, like who she was fucking.

"But, none of your jackets matched my purses."

Seriously? She has to be joking. I'm going to take that as a joke. It is such a fucking shame, the way American ideal works...why is it that no one's opinion is more important than that of an attractive person? Vanity is the ruler of people's decision making. Fuck it, she wants to play. Then, I'll play too. Who cares about love anyway? The shit isn't real...it can't be real. It was mentioned in the bible for Christ sake.

"Who else has made you squirt?"

Alexia's face turned beet red and I could sense that she wanted to punch me, out of both love and anger.

"Damn, you sure did. I forgot you did that."

I felt my chest drop and butterflies flutter in my abdomen. Wow, she had forgotten that I had made her. I suppose she really did forget about you. Damn you and your thoughts.

"How in the fuck you gonna forget?" I asked.

On the inside I was irate. My body felt like it was going to explode due to the ire that was welling within it.

"I didn't mean to forget! I just pushed you out of my mind. Now I'm thinking about the shit."

My body cooled a bit and I relaxed, soothed a bit by her answer. Still, I dare not believe a word she utters. How could I? Why would I? The animalistic lust for her goes extremely well with my unquenchable need. Yet all I can do is reminisce.

"Yeah, yeah. Tell me anything bruh. You didn't answer my question though," I said.

"Nobody, nigga. Damn. Change the subject man...what else have you been doing? You still in school?" She asked, visibly annoyed.

"I graduated in May, I'll go back to get my masters soon and, eventually you'll be speaking to a Doctor of Communication. I had an interview with GCS recently, for a news-writing position. Journalism is cool but I think I'd be better suited writing books and..." I hesitated. I reclined in my chair, only to be tipped forward. I turned around to see the waitress standing over me with a scowl on her face.

"Don't lean back, I ain't responsible," the waitress said.

I gave the waitress a wild look and was met with an equal one back. Fuck, this is a tough lady.

I was a little perturbed by how forward she was, so I turned and noticed a bowl of Sake sitting in front of me. This motherfucking lady must be some type of genie or a fucking ninja. Lord have mercy, Las Vegas has characters everywhere. This is insane.

"Lady, you don't have to be so rude. We didn't drop the

drinks, but we are still thankful that you brought us some out. Thank you," Alexia said.

"It's ok sweetie. It's just that asshole of a fucking chef. He's my son. Santi is his godfather. Holler if you need me."

On cue, the Compton chef came sauntering in. Being a person that enjoys a cocaine induced high from time to time, I have enough expertise in sensing when a person is high and when one is not. Jeffrey looked as if he had tooted some shit straight from motherfucking Colombia. I looked at him and then at Alexia while she eyed the menu.

I gazed at her smooth skin; small freckles dotting the sides of her face racing up to her nose & I wondered how the night would end. I tried to create a small window of opportunity that would allow me to keep this feeling around. Sometimes, as a person, a man is set to do certain things that even he can't fathom, simply because he thinks of them. I wonder if this is one of those nights.

"Look asshole," the waitress growled, grabbing the all-star chef by the front of his shirt.

"Don't fuck up, and be fucking professional. Asshole, these are Santi's people. Don't fuck up, or I'll use you as fucking steak."

His eyes bulged out of his head and his pupils were big as dinner plates. I wondered how he was set to cook our food. Fuck it, I've cooked some of my best meals destroyed off of my ass, I'm sure this prick can whip himself some bullshit meal.

"Damn Ma, you a crazy sadistic ass ain't you? Look, peace out and bring some drink when I whistle."

"Fuck you Jeffrey. I should have named you Sherman. Nerd bitch."

Alexia looked at me and burst into laughter.

Oh really? This shit was funny to her. Her laughter wasn't a contrived laughter either. It was a real laughter, one that was deep and echoed. A real heart felt piece of shit collaboration of sound from some stupid ass vocal chords.

"Fuck you…"

I couldn't think of anything else to say to the little short woman. I was pissed. Who in the flying fuck does she think she is?

"Fuck you lady. My name is Sherman. My real name. Fuck you," I said.

"Well look here you little ne…"

"Hold on, you stupid….," Alexia chimed, visibly upset. She

now stood and faced the waitress. "Stop your mouth. You've been insulting, so get your stupid ass on. I'm in a dress but I will beat you up and then eat your son's food. And not tip him."

The waitress, huffed and puffed and disappeared into the abyss of another man's emotion.

I'm glad our food doesn't have to go into the back… It's nice to have Alexia here…I miss that…I miss the nights that we had, running amuck at Big Teds, acting as if tomorrow was never coming. We had our fun together and that is something that I will always miss.

Jeffrey stood behind the grill, miserable and broken. Good food is made with love. How in the hell can I pep this guy up?

"Yo Compton, you good? You wanna see some titties?" I said, grabbing Alexia's left boob. "Here you go bro, she's about to show you."

"Dude!"

At least she's laughing and not screaming. I'm cool.

"Dude, you gotta stop! I can't stand you," Alexia laughed, her face lit up.

I gazed at her momentarily, her beauty striking me. I felt as a young boy did when his father chastised him; helpless. It is a pain when you are stricken by something reflecting such vanity. It is even worse when you love the appearance of something as well as the make-up of the thing…you love what it is, in all of its actuality. What is love? Who knows?

Alexia grabbed my hand and removed it from her breast. The chef cracked a smile. Very good… I was glad that he had a smile on his face. Smiles are always great, even though some people are extremely twisted and smile at the sight of horrific incidents.

"So, I know it's none of my business but I mean shit…" I said.

"What? You want to know who fucks me…huh?"

I gawked at her, rolled my eyes, and poured a shot of sake for both of us. She raised her shot glass to her nose and sniffed, the tip of her nose got wet. We both giggled, and she wiped the sake from her face, leaned her head back and drank. Alexia was the type of woman that made you want to do bad things with her. Good thing, because if she makes me laugh again, we're probably going to have to get naked. I poured us each another shot, and then another.

"You're trying to have a little confessional tonight aren't you!"

Alexia leaned her head and took her third sake shot.

I really enjoy sake. Everyone enjoys sake. It's a creeper that takes hold of you, sort of like a seductive woman…slowly and sensually, ever so gracefully caressing you until you are under her spell and doing whatever she may ask of you.

Jeffrey wasn't doing anything but looking at us, smiling, bug eyed with pupils the size of dinner plates. Once Alexia sat her glass down, he spoke.

"Look cuz, Santi told moms to give y'all anything ya wanted. Ima just cook everything cuz."

Jeffrey grabbed a bottle of clear liquid and squirt it on the hibachi grill and lit it on fire.

"Yo, I'm high as you can tell and I ain't really trying to do all of those stupid ass tricks like I be doing to them fools in the main part."

Alexia and I looked at each other and then at Jeffrey, both of us with the same perplexed expression.

"What you niggas don't want to eat good? Lucky I'm not trying to get my ass kicked."

Grabbing Alexia's shot glass; I muttered "we're due for another shot" while wondering how many calories this sake is going to add to my daily consumption. I need to know how many I burn while running from my emotions. I know exactly where this night is going to lead. I just hope that I am prepared to go through what I am bound to go through once Alexia and I part ways. Maybe I could go with her to Los Angeles…

"Bottoms up."

Alexia raised her shot glass and I followed, clanking mine into hers.

Time seemed to be standing still while I was with her. Time crept as I sat with Alexia. I felt like I was in some bad religion, a cosmic terror of horror. When we were together, she made it easy for me to operate in this dark and inhospitable shit hole of a world. I know that it will flee though. It wasn't meant to last. It was meant to teach me a lesson; leave well enough alone.

"What were you saying earlier?" I asked Alexia, grabbing the outside of each of her thighs, turning her body towards me. I placed my right hand on her left knee and gently moved it up her thigh, scooting in her direction from my chair.

"Who I'm fucking?" Alexia tested.

"Yeah, I guess you were going to tell me that. It really doesn't matter. None of my business. I'm not trying to know...."

Alexia grabbed my hand and tossed it onto my lap.

"Don't start," she mumbled and turned to face the grill. "I didn't come here to be on a guilt trip."

She didn't want to be on a guilt trip and I didn't want her to be on one.

Jeffery raised his head from his cooking. He was removing the shell from the lobster tail. Alexia glared at me. I remembered the look from my past vividly. She had the ability to make her eyes turn evil. I had room to get upset however. I had done my share of dirt long before this had happened. Although, so had she. Regardless, it is odd how human-beings work. Many times, people wed others knowing that their significant other has had intercourse with someone that they know. Everyone fucks everyone. It is pretty fucking disgusting to be completely honest.

"You know what, I just realized that I don't even like you for real."

I can't believe that I just said that. And it wasn't the drugs talking. Hell no. That was real. That was a real emotion being emoted through real words. I actually felt that...but did I want to feel it? Regardless, it had happened. I had felt it.

It's so cool, how life will teach you to understand the obstinate instant between being forced through a vaginal canal or pulled through a belly incision and being buried six feet deep or cremated and tossed into the ocean.

"Why are you looking like that?" I asked

Alexia's face looked like someone etched it out of marble; stone cold and beautiful. I didn't understand why she was upset.

"It's beginning to look a lot like fuck this and fuck you," Alexia said angrily. "You constantly bring up shit that happened, instead of worrying about right now. Worry about today for once in your life. Shit happens dude, can't change a damn thing. You fucked girls that I was cool with when I was running around acting like you were it. I grew up dude, fuck what you talking about."

Alexia began to stand but I grabbed her wrist and sat her back into her chair. At the moment that anyone is doing anything, they believe that the rationale that they have formulated in their minds is correct and not faulty. She believed that she was right in what she did. I believed I was correct in this instance. I suppose that at the very root of it all, both of our actions were free from attachment of the outcome, on the surface. In reality, we were both very much attached to the outcome…bringing us to this point. My statement, her anger…yet and still, grabbing her wrist and looking into her eyes, I hoped that she felt what I was feeling…a warm embrace from and by the uncertain…all possibilities.

"I fucking love the way you say things back to me, especially when I say some bullshit to you first," I said.

I didn't really know what to say. But hell, I'm eating dinner with her ass in Las Vegas. I swear I'm like Jesus, except I only forgive smoking hot women.

Alexia relaxed as I eased my light grip from her wrist. I poured each of us another shot of sake and gently placed hers in her hand. Sake is a hell of an alcohol. It will sneak up on you and turn you into a loving creature from a mythical forest or a demonic heathen from the land of fuck-your-mother. Drinking this stuff with women is extremely dangerous as well…you never know what is going to happen.

I'm glad Alexia can consume alcohol though… Dealing with her, I've realized a lot about drinkers:

If they get a hangover, they are not real alcoholics and they shouldn't be trusted. I trust people who get hangovers just about as much as I trust a person that eats ham and pineapple pizza.

Alexia and I took our shots of sake as Jeffrey asked us how we wanted our steak cooked. Alexia finished her shot before me, yelping a "well done" to Jeffrey. I set my glass down to see Jeffrey give Alexia a side eye from hell. I was perturbed as well, a repulsion welling inside of my physical being for what I have just heard. Well done? What in the flying fuck? I live by the rule that if a woman orders any type of steak to be cooked well done, she has to pay for it herself. I'm pissed.

"Well done?"

I couldn't help but look at Alexia and repeat her statement to her in the form of a question. Well done?

I looked to Jeffrey and told him to cook the steak medium rare. I turned my head back to Alexia only to be hit with a large grin. She knew me well enough to know that I considered anyone that so much as contemplated a well done red meat to be a devil.

"I wasn't gonna make this shit well done anyway," Jeffrey remarked without looking up, his focus on slicing, dicing and flipping vegetables. His heart was beating a mile a minute with all of the cocaine that he snorted, "Well done steak…. People who eat that shit are toilet paper, making shitty life decisions."

Alexia burst into intense laughter, nearly falling out of her seat. The sake had gotten to her. Any other time I would tell her to slow down, but we're in Vegas. Enjoy the fucking ride.

"Hey, dude… when you gonna be finished with the food? A bitch is starving!" Alexia yelled and smiled at the chef.

Instantly, like a fucking ninja, a swift left hand grabbed my shot glass that was subsequently filled by a right hand. Perfectly manicured, her hands gripped the glass and kettle elegantly. She filled both of our shot glasses and set the kettle down, all the while staring at me intently.

"Drink up."

We each tossed the grain liquor into our mouths and she re-filled both glasses.

"You're one of those people who wasn't spanked a lot as a kid, ain't you?" Jeffrey asked Alexia, as he placed rice onto her plate. His face wasn't pleasant anymore. I could tell that he was in dire need of alcohol or more blow.

Jeffrey continued to pile food onto both of our plates; a smorgasbord of various meats and vegetables. Squash and artichoke never crossed my mind as being remotely edible until I ventured to a hibachi restaurant for the first time.

"You better finish that food," Alexia said, mean-mugging the chef. Jeffrey stood silent, but visibly frustrated. It is quite funny, how she has managed to upset both the hostess and chef. She was a handful of fire, and alcohol only made it worse. "Why you look so evil? Life is good as shit man."

I glanced to Jeffrey and noticed that his face was red.

"Well, I look evil because I am evil. Do you have any more stupid ass questions?"

"Maybe you're so mad because you're a turd and can't be on team YOLO," She said with her head down and hovered over her plate as a vulture would over a carcass.

"They never brought out the egg soup," she exclaimed, shoving a mouthful of rice and shrimp into her mouth. "It's cool though. How'd you get this back room anyway?"

The walls of the room were filled with beautiful decorations, numerous pictures, and statues. Looking at the ornaments and figures on the walls give you a sense of prestige. Pictures of the Flower of Life and the lotus, effervescent and embodying everything geometrical with the universe and ourselves as simply as we can be yet connected to everything around us, gave me a feeling of love and admiration of myself and my own strength; I know who I am and what I am and what I shall be and do in the future. There, seated and observing, I came to grips with the imperfection that is perfect. Nothing lasts; nothing is perfect; nothing is finished.

The unique nature of Alexia, as simply an aesthetic, is beautiful because it is imperfect. Eating as a hound would with the appearance of a goddess, working in the pornographic industry in order to fund her career as a lawyer. She is the epitome of flawed beauty, the epicenter of my own quietness; A stupendous anomaly. Yet, seated in observation, one cannot help but to surrender to the reality that this life is mine.

It's a simple equation to me...one snort of cocaine into my nose equates to your inspiration. Why? Because this cocaine isn't going to snort itself. When a person is experiencing or holding a piece of joy and love, they vibrate at a level so high... a frequency so advanced and elevated, that it affects everyone and everything around them. It oscillates and moves outward, effecting infinitely. So much fucking love floating around that you can't breathe, that's how much love I'm giving off.

"You have to appreciate every single moment that God gives you," I said with glassy eyed apathy.

"What does that have to do with you getting this room?" Alexia said as rice and shrimp fell out of her mouth. I couldn't help but raise my eyebrows in pure astonishment at this gorgeous woman eating as if she was a hog in a barn. The sight of it is pretty disgusting and my brain was wrecking trying to figure out why in the fuck she is trying to be interesting. It must be exhausting.

"Nothing. Nothing."

I eyed my food, a sickening spell befalling me...partly due to Alexia's eating habits and partly due to an empty stomach and a shitload of sake. I was utterly amazed that a woman so aesthetically beautiful could eat in such an ugly fashion. I wanted to question it, partly due to the fact that past memories do not include her eating as a savage would and partly because who in the hell wouldn't ask a person why they are eating as if they were a Neanderthal. I've never tried to forget the memories that Alexia and I have shared. It would be ridiculous and counter-productive anyway. Memories are trick birthday candles; one second you think you've exterminated it and the next, the flame is bright as ever.

My addiction to her wouldn't let me cringe for too long however. Sitting there, eating as disgusting as she was, I still found her beautiful. Wabi-Sabi. I was told long ago that the strongest drug that exists for a person is another person, and it could not be truer. A person will go through hell in order to be with another, similar to a person destroying themselves over a 5-minute high. I wanted to be around her and feel her presence, even though everything in, of, and around me warned not to delve into the nether regions of undying love; the dark and indefinite longing that is home.

I understand that time heals most anything and pain is something that cannot be escaped, however being drunken works instantaneously, and has the copious capacity to eradicate the rationalization that was the cause of discomfort in the first place. And drunk I was. It's rather joyous and endearing when you find a person that you can take to visit your demons, even if it is so your demons will have company. While they are enamored with their demons frolicking freely with your own, you can stealthily trap their destiny in a bottle. You know what I find intriguing? The fact that we do not know what we want in or out of life, yet are responsible for who and what we are. It is one of the most fucked up state of affairs of being a human. From the past to the present to the future, we change our minds repeatedly, always desiring something different. There should be no wonder why we are so tense…and this fact; dealing with others and their bullshit, brings me to the grim realization that I am destined to walk a lonely road. This is where my life is going. Life fucked me hard and dared not call back. I know that everything will be alright however, I just don't know when.

"What if I told you that I loved you more than life itself?" Alexia asked, eyes glazed by her devilish intake of sake.

"What the fuck?" I replied, visibly confused by the words that she chose to expel. She shot back a look of despair and sadness. Why in the hell does she look like that and why did she ask me that question? "Well, I'd probably ask if you were suicidal."

"Fuck you then," Alexia retorted, pouring another sake shot. "You want one. Yeah fuck you, you do."

"You getting me drunk? What if I don't want to have sex with you?" I asked.

"You'd better," replied Alexia.

"I'd better what?"

"Don't be ignorant," She said, sliding a shot glass to me. "Cheers."

She raised her glass towards me and after several seconds of eyeing Alexia, I reluctantly grabbed my glass and raised it towards hers.

"...To love! To life! To everything ever hoped for!" Alexia's voice rang, startling Jeffrey as he cleaned the grill. He eyed her grimly and I assumed that he secretly wanted to kill her, and possibly would have if I hadn't of slid him a $50 bill wrapped tightly around a half gram of cocaine.

Looking briefly at the bill and then to me, I wiggled my nose as if I were a fluffy bunny rabbit...or armless with a rough case of allergies. This gesture is universal in the realm of powder users. He grinned as I motioned for him to exit the room, skipping away like a six-year-old girl during recess.

"Mother of God, I am glad that shit head left. You still haven't told me how you got this room? Who do you know?"

"Heaven."

"Are you serious?" she asked, eyebrows raised.

"Yes. I am very serious. I initially came to Vegas in order to act in the manner of a hooligan for Shelby's bachelor party weekend, but all of that changed once we boarded the plane."

Alexia eyed me with confusion, her face ruffling in such a way that I knew what she was about to say.

"What the fuck?"

"Look, girl...We boarded a plane, met a flight attendant, and my world has pretty much been turned upside down since. Between the guns and drugs and threats to my life, I'm not sure what the fuck is going on. Besides that, I've still acted like a hooligan...so all hasn't been lost."

"What in the fuck are you talking about?" she asked.

I sat squarely in my chair and turned towards her, my eyes nearly shut. My cocaine-levels were low. I sat there resting my eyes for several seconds, calming myself...gaining composure. Then I felt cold hands wrap around my cheeks...chill and supple.

"Well, fuck this Heaven thing. You're out of it. You just told me to come. How has Shelby been anyway?"

I didn't want to expound upon knowing Heaven or even how I was tricked into searching for it…them. As I opened my eyes, I turned forward to face my plate of food and noticed the uneven natural wood paneling of the walls. The imperfections were holy; everything fit. As I stared at the walls details, I contemplated this trip, and it began to make sense. Melody was the catalyst for the majority of my latest experiences. Persuading me to search for Heaven had surely created the means for a grandiose escapade through Las Vegas. It baffled me as to how and why I was chosen to know Heaven. It is even more baffling that the leader of Heaven initially found me. I wonder what Melody is doing right now…is she thinking about me? The amazement of something fresh and new, something so different from what you know and are used to is a magnetic force. On our escapade that I barely remembered, I had found that her favorite meal was chicken tenders and fries, and that she also drove Porsche. It was confusing, and I am in love. But this love feels different from the love I have for Alexia. It is not murky or tainted by disturbing emotions and thoughts of past antics. It is not a scar that I have grown to love. No, this love is perfect.

"Shel's good," I mumbled, my stomach tightening with hunger. "I can't believe dude is getting married. Shit's wild."

"I know! Maaaan…I think about us a lot. We should be, could be…," Alexia's voice waned as she spoke, her body leaning back and head lifting to the sky in contemplation. She gave a deep sigh, likely thinking of the awesomeness that she lost when she left me. I was too busy wondering about the awesomeness that I was set to give, to Melody. We sat in silence for a while, the only sounds coming from the patter of my fork on the plate and text message sounds from her cell phone.

"You know; we could work if you promise to only stay as long as I don't need you. You make me weak…when I begin to feel attached, I need for you to be gone," I said.

Alexia's head quickly rose from her cell phone to reveal a puzzled expression, one that became even more perplexed as I reached into my pocket to retrieve a buzzing cell phone. I've never answered a cell phone call or text message while out on dates with Alexia, yet this habit was inadvertently broken upon her abrupt departure from me. She didn't speak, and instead drooped her shoulders in defeat. She cupped her right hand with her left and placed them into her lap. I noticed her dejection and quickly concluded that it was none of my fucking business. I was filled with joy by the voice on the other end of the phone, its sultry tone causing elation inside of me, reminiscent of a 14-year-old Sherman on the verge of losing his virginity. My stomach fluttered in nervousness as the voice on the other end spoke, and my face reflected this anxiety with a weary smile. Her words were everything that I wanted to hear; the directions to a soul lost on a journey for the reclamation of love. I continued smiling as our conversation ended, looking down at the phone for several seconds before turning to Alexia.

"Hey, I have to go to the restroom,"

I rose from the table and began to exit our dining area when Jeffrey and his mother entered the room. They both smirked when they saw me, Jeffrey giving a side eye and his mother nodding her head. I looked back to Alexia, her head low reflecting a state of loneliness that would probably equate to her departure from the restaurant while I was away in the restroom. Sure, I felt bad for what I was about to do, but history is perpetual and the tables often turn. The oddity of romantic relationships is that they should not and are not all about sexual pleasure. Sex was what it was about the entire time.... I had to flee, it would be the righteous thing to do. Alexia, albeit a friend since childhood...I had to let her go. I had to leave and never hear from her again. Fuck it. Hopefully it doesn't come back to bite me in the ass. I always try to crawl through open doors and the universe always closes my fingers in it...God has a crude sense of humor.

Entering into the main dining area of the restaurant, I inquired from a hostess the whereabouts of the restroom. The gods are with me tonight...this is supposed to happen. I strutted to it, head high and chest puffed as if I metamorphosed into a show horse. I didn't bother entering into it though; I instead gently pushed the door open, took two steps inside and turned and exited. Fuck going into the restroom...I'm out of here. I allowed her to rip my soul into pieces of nothingness once before and it shan't happen again. The human mind is a mysterious machine. It allows us to recall some memories while other things are treated as if they never occurred. The negative episodes that our passionate and tumultuous relationship was built on flooded my mind as the breaching of a dam would a city. Luckily, the restroom was situated at the front of the restaurant near the exit, so it took only six steps to make my way outside. I kept my head down as I walked out of the building, and was stunned upon my exit...

Sitting in front of me was the most gorgeous duo that I have ever laid eyes on. A stretch limousine sat idled underneath the valet canopy of Smith as Melody stood through its moon roof, screaming at the top of her lungs. She held a bottle of champagne in one hand and a blunt in the other high above her head. The sight was magical and fantastic, affording me the feeling one may get from seeing an angel in the flesh.

"I wish I had a fucking audience man," Melody yelled, straining over the engine. "I'm never on time. And here I am, on time, and no one is here to appreciate it!"

I walked towards the vehicle, enamored with the elegance that was in front of me.

"Hurry the fuck up! We got shit to get to motherfucker," She screamed.

A door to the limo opened and Katy Perry blared as numerous people sang along. I hesitated, and then climbed into the limo, not knowing what type of fuckery I was set to get myself into. I've always been weary of entering limousines filled with drunk and ferocious people, however with Melody screaming at me to enter, I'll be damned if I miss this shit.

What I saw next sent chills through my spine and excited me to no end. My brother, Corey, and two of my closest friends sat around, wide eyed and cocaine crazed. They were each in their own worlds, chatting and screaming and laughing, spraying champagne and spilling alcohol from bottles. Each man dressed in suits, they appeared as rabid as hyena's but were as playful as puppies. I had not seen Dover nor Darnell for over a year, so it pleased me to have them along on my quest to find Heaven. As the hours roll, the further from Heaven I feel that I am from, yet the people that I would want with me in Heaven, are here. I have found it.

"Welcome back to sanity motherfucker!" screamed one of my friends.

Melody reached for my hand and pulled me to the rear of the limousine and sat on my lap, but not before I slapped 'fives' with everyone and gave a grand salutation.

"What's up motherfuckerrrrrs!" I yelled, holding two middle fingers in the air.

I couldn't be happier….and I felt the joy of right now well inside of my chest. A number of beautiful women, dressed in luxurious cocktail gowns and party dresses filled the rest of the seats in the limousine. All held champagne glasses, except for one. She sat next to my brother, holding a bottle, drinking from it freely. I noticed that Shelby had his right arm around her waist as they sat next to one another, and he held a matching bottle of champagne in his left.

All of the women present possessed daunting beauty; aesthetically they each would intimidate and over-shadow most other women, yet they were comfortable around each other, and I wondered if they had been hired as escorts or plucked off of the street near one of the many colossal hotels populating Las Vegas Boulevard.

Dover, who happened to be a substance abuse official for the largest drug and alcohol addiction center in the St. Louis area, stood and waddled his way towards me from the other end of the limo. As he walked he spilled champagne over several lady's high heels and feet.

"Long time no see motherfucker," Dover said while pitching me a walnut sized rock of cocaine. "I took this shit from a guy at the job earlier today. It's crazy the shit you get away with wearing a badge."

I looked at him with a wide eyed grin and opened the bag. He sat next to Melody and I, giggling as I eased her off of my lap in order to more easily powder my nose. Darnell sat about four feet from us, feet kicked up tongue kissing a Korean woman. Unexpectedly, Darnell jerked and tossed the woman from his lap and grabbed his bottle of champagne, turning it up to his face and guzzling the remainder.

"Aye turn that shit the fuck up!" Darnell yelled to the driver. "Nigga this is my shit! Sherm, drink up nigga!"

Ecstatic isn't a strong enough word to describe the way that I feel. There's nothing like Las Vegas. Jesus died for our sins after all. If you don't sin, he died for nothing.

SUNDAY, 6:48 A.M. PST

25 miles outside of San Bernardino, I had an epiphany...

Life is too gorgeous to waste wallowing in its filth; The filth, created by us, will make you feel more of a pig than you actually are. Life is glorious and wonderful, and if it weren't for the tremendous amount of cocaine and alcohol coursing through my body, I'd still be elated. It's too late to turn back now, so I told Melody to floor the gas pedal on the 1967 Ford Mustang that we had apparently commandeered earlier in the night. I don't remember much of anything beyond the fourth bottle of tequila that Dover purchased while we partied, except for a near mishap of epic proportions.

~

Darnell had disappeared two hours into the function; apparently he succumbed to the detriment that alcohol and cocaine provided and had passed out in the club restroom. No one seemed to notice that he was missing however. The poor devil.

He had just returned to the States after being on a year-long excursion in Senegal in an attempt to capture a prized group of Rhesus monkeys, whom had escaped from a make-shift research laboratory deep in the jungle, at which he was at the helm of. An expert and doctor in primate psychology, he spent years grooming and caring for these Rhesus', raising them into monstrosity's hell bent on terrorizing every living organism they came into contact with, to the verge of suicide.

On a bright morning, three members of his research team, students from a prestigious European university, ventured off with the camp guide, a local crab sorcerer named Baba. They were in search of edible fruits and berries but decided to fish in a nearby river and scout several acres of land for various troubles. Three days passed as Darnell's worry grew to angst and frustration, and with no sign of his crew, he feared the worst...maybe they had been eaten by giant cockroaches imported from Madagascar, the hideous creatures. "Death Bugs", as they are aptly named, gave

Darnell the fright of his young adult life as he witnessed a hoard of the fanged and winged demons…9 inches in length and 4 inches wide, devour half of the carcass of a crocodile that had been split in two during an epic battle with a hippopotamus, while he was visiting a zoo in South Africa.

Three whole days later, Baba and the three imbeciles returned to the research site covered in mud and blood, and smelling of feces and urine. One of the students, a female, was missing an eye while another, a scrawny guy with curly brown hair, sported tennis ball sized boils all over his body. The boils had stretched his skin so tightly that they were red as a Cardinal bird. In addition, they oozed pus, even the abscess that protruded from the middle of his head, as if he were a pubescent unicorn. The site of the monstrous lump provided Darnell with the taste of vomit as it pulsed and secreted…he was disgusted and thought the poor soul's ailment was so vile that he debated killing him and feeding his body to warthogs. Seven teeth were also missing from this student's mouth, the result of a fight with the human dental structure and a gigantic rock.

The students told Darnell of a disgusting drink created from a local plant. Deeper and deeper down the rabbit hole Baba led, deeper and deeper into the jungle they went, as he told of how he first came into contact with the devils weed many, many, years ago. Eventually they came across the plant and with his aid, all hell broke loose. The male student said that after drinking the concoction brewed by Baba, they felt as if they were living in the worst nightmare that they had ever experienced.

Baba laughed cruelly when they mentioned this, and spoke only a few words about his disdain for them and that the students would be cursed forever. He also stated that the Rhesus monkeys had been killed by some sort of predatory bird. Darnell didn't show a sign of anger over the incident…no anger besides that which stemmed from becoming aware of a village that was home to 3 dozen orphaned children being decimated by the three Oxford students. Darnell never found out the God-forsaken reason why his brightest students decided to be participants to one of the most powerful hallucinogens known to modern man, however he had grounds to believe that the unborn leader of the monkey clan hypnotized the students and tricked them into it. These events were the motivation for Darnell's desire to be as equal to nothingness as possible, whilst canoodling in Las Vegas.

Security found and escorted Darnell to a band of Clark County Sheriff's that were posted outside of the club's entrance and miraculously, as God and the universe had truly intended, Dover and I stumbled out of the club and through the lobby of the hotel, right out of the revolving doors to witness Darnell being stuffed into the back of a cop car.

"Darnell we've been looking for you all fucking night! Where the fuck you been?!" I yelled to him.

"Maaan they kidnapped me!" Darnell screeched, as two sheriff's deputies held his head and made attempts to shove him into the back seat.

Dover and I began racing towards him, yelling at the officers to release him. Darnell dropped to his knees, stalling the deputies from pushing him further into the patrol car.

"Officer!" I screamed, reaching the patrol car, eyes bloodshot red and face sweating profusely.

"Santiago Mora will have your fucking head!"

Five minutes later we were back inside of the club, tooting lines off of bathroom stall toilet paper dispensers.

~

Hurling down the 605 at speeds rivaling that of a NASCAR driver, light from the dawning sun stinging my eyes like bites from fire ants to the stomping feet of an ignorant child desecrating their hill, I realized that it was too late to turn back. Who in the hell did I think that I was? Stealing a fucking Mustang from a hapless dope at a gas station…it was all Melody's fault. I tell you, beauty disguises the most devilish beings. The mountains…they were beautiful, and like Melody, deathly if you had not a clue as to how to survive within them, and all of the elements and surprises that they may bring. The mountain is a call girl, a prostitute that is always there to give you the most thrilling time of your life. But she may steal your soul whilst engaging you, and you'll never be able to tell your story again.

What is it that a man yearns for? Is it not money? Is it not pride? I feel that it cannot and shan't be. It is a coy…something ego driven…a mask. Men seek love. Men seek affection. Men need it. It is an innate necessity essential to and in all Men. It is as if a portion of you cannot complete until it has tasted that incredible feeling…one of exuberance and jubilee, that which fills you up and makes you want to explode. It is a wondrous feeling, almost indescribable; it isn't something that words can express. It's real. And it's the only tangible thing that truly exists.

Arguments often occur due to the absurd reasoning that there are different types of love. At times I too lean toward this perception, yet I am often carried back into the realization that love is what it is, on any level. It all revolves around the same premise, whatever you would like to call it; awareness, paying attention.

I looked to my left at Melody, the sun slowly rising behind the left side of her head.

"Hopefully we make it to see the sunrise," She said.

She peered at the road ahead, the bottom of her wrist tucked over the top of the steering wheel. Melody was beautiful. For the first time, I noticed how beautiful her bronze skin was as it glistened in the light shining through the window. A Koi fish was etched in ink on her right arm. She also had 'carpe diem' on her right wrist. These tattoos were something that I had never noticed before, and the sight of them made me smile.

"Hey, check the glove box. Santi usually keeps weed in here," Melody said, motioning to the glove compartment.

I looked at Melody perplexed, my smile turning into a twisted snarl of confusion.

"Santi? This is his car? So what in the fuck was all of that shit back there for!?"

"Dude, just check the fucking glove box. I'll tell you once you smoke and calm down. You're fucking wired."

This woman kept me twisting and turning. I knew that she was dangerous…she was no good. She was a wonderful person, seemingly loyal and extremely intelligent, however she was as crooked as a two-year-old spelling their name, and I was intrigued by it.

"Are you some type of ninja? A secret agent? Hell, I'm starting to believe that you're a fucking super hero," I asked as I opened the glove box. I had enough alcohol and cocaine coursing through my body to resurrect a two-week old dead man, so I did as I was told.

Melody didn't answer, but an eerie grin slid across her face.

"Is any in there?"

"No, only a box," I replied.

"That's it. Roll up fool!" Melody let out a robust laugh, her smile brightening the entire vehicle.

I grabbed the box, nearly dropping it onto the floor from the weight of it. What the fuck? How much weed does he keep in this thing?

Opening the box revealed a half ounce of marijuana, three cigarillos, and a .45 caliber revolver. We're headed to California with a gun…great. I'm pretty sure that Melody is a felon, seeing that she's hooked up with so many crooks. I didn't bother asking about the weapon due to not wanting to seem like a little bitch, so I instead acted like it wasn't in my sight. I was surprised that the smell of pot didn't singe my nose hairs once I opened the bag and squeezed a bud. A smile formed on my face as the smell of ganja wafted the air. I shut the box and began to break down the buds that I had retrieved, my fingers sticking together like I had played in glue.

"Holy shit, what in the fuck is this?" I asked.

"It's my strain…I made it. We're headed to my beach house anyway. I'll show you."

"I'll need you to fly some of this shit to Louisville," I mumbled, licking the cigarillo closed. "Got a lighter?"

"Look in my purse it's in the backseat," Melody replied.

"No," I responded emphatically.

Melody looked at me awkwardly, her eyes squinted as if I had just let out a disgusting fart.

"You can look into my purse. I know men aren't supposed to do so, but I'm driving and wanna smoke. Grab it."

I looked at her for several seconds, debating whether I was going to reach into her purse and rummage for a lighter or make her pull over onto the side of the highway and retrieve it herself. Just as she was about to open her mouth, probably to curse me in a way that I had never been cursed before, I put the stash box into the glove compartment and turned around to grab the purse. "What the fucks in here?"

"Nothing, why?"

"Cause it doesn't feel like anything's in here," I said sarcastically.

Setting the purse on my lap, the lighter was the first thing that I saw which made me ecstatic. I for damned sure had no desire to finagle the inside of a handbag. I sat the purse on the car floor, put the blunt to my lips and struck the lighter, the flame vivifying Melody and I.

"What in the fuck!"

I took one drag of the blunt and nearly coughed up a lung. My face began to sweat and mouth began to water as tears streamed down my eyes. I hacked uncontrollably, my lungs making a desperate attempt to keep as much oxygen inside of my body as possible. This terribleness went on for so long that the blunt needed to be re-lit. Melody giggled excessively as I was nearly a victim of asphyxiation by smoke inhalation. I again lit the blunt, yet was unable to control myself enough so that I could actually enjoy what I was smoking. Thoughts began to fly around my head and then out of it. She grew this? Good lord. The confusion that had mounted within me weighed heavy. Who and what is she?

"But yeah," Melody stated, "I can get whatever you need there. What kind of volume are you looking for? The demand is insane in Kentucky. I couldn't keep up with Primetime."

"Primetime? He's from Kentucky?"

"Yep. Cornbread," She replied.

My mouth dropped. Had my dreams come true? In searching for Heaven, it seemed that I had actually found it in the most unlikely of places. Santiago's words, those that he spoke after we departed during our initial meeting, rang loudly as ever.... "Searching for water in hell, you meet the strangest people."

Melody continued speaking, hitting the blunt between each word.

"That's why he's out here now. I gave my dad to him," She passed the blunt to me, blowing smoke into my face in the process.

"So that explains you beating that guy with the baton at the gas station right," I said. The situation in itself was bizarre. I've never witnessed a grown man turn into a puppy. I've also never witnessed a grown man running wildly through a convenience store, screaming for mercy at the top of his lungs. I just hope that the rental car sitting at the gas station doesn't come back to me.

It didn't surprise me that Santi was Melody's father; they both were twisted as ever. She had probably been his saving grace at one point, helping him to gain innumerable hoard's of cash in a variety of ways.

"Roll another,"

I looked at Melody and turned my nose up once again. I wanted to know why in the fuck she did what she did and why in the fuck I had to be involved in it. The answer was simple however. As a youth, I was taught that if you are with someone high on your personal totem pole of friendship, and they happen to become engaged in a physical disagreement or mishap, you inherit that physical disagreement. Would you want the person that you are with to turn the blind eye while you get your ass beat? I certainly would hope not…

"Matter of fact, roll both of them…We're nearly to Venice," Melody piped, staring straight ahead. As I rolled, she drove and eventually my frustration dissipated. Driving for four hours with no sound had nearly driven me insane. Once I finished my marijuana project, I reached left and turned on the radio. Slowly rotating the dial first to the left and then to the far right, I began to hear violins and clarinets and suddenly I was thrust into direct nostalgia of 1967. "What a Wonderful World" by Louis Armstrong streamed from the speakers like a ribbon would in the wind, and I smiled. I became warm and relaxed, realizing that anything that had taken place was not my issue, even though I had a minute involvement in it. Everything was good…and Melody was here with me. I increased the volume on the radio, leaned my seat back and lit the second of our three blunts…Cruising the freeway with a devil in a mini skirt, windows down…the world was indeed wonderful.

SUNDAY, 7:49 A.M. PST

"I'm surprised that you even picked up on what was going on. You don't seem like that type of guy," Melody said as she blew smoke from her mouth, arms wrapped around as she hugged herself. The salty chill of the light Pacific Ocean breeze blew against us as we walked down Venice Beach, my suit jacket draping her shoulders and flowing with the air in the same fashion of her hair. The setting was as beautiful as anything that I ever had the blessing of witnessing, and a joy rose inside of me. I gazed, first at Melody and then at the sun during its rise. Purple and orange hues painted the bottom of the horizon as the sun rose from behind the shimmering ocean and into the sky, reflecting handsomely onto the water's surface.

"There are a lot of things that you wouldn't assume about me, however you shouldn't judge…" I said.

"Yeah, I know. I figure that you're pretty fucking wild anyway, sniffing coke on an airplane full of people and all."

We both chuckled. Walking in the sand barefoot as daylight rises, hand in hand, enjoying the company that the full breadth of communication enables is one of the most fulfilling activities one can engage. With each step that I took, my toes pressed solidly into the cold, damp sand and molded perfectly to the contour of my feet. I noticed how the sand squeezed between the creases of my toes and rolled over top of them as if the earth were attempting to envelope me. Oddly enough, a strange sense of security overcame me, and as I looked at Melody smoking the last blunt, I was unable to hold my joy. I had never in life possessed the feeling that I currently held, nor had I ever felt as strongly about a person in such a short amount of time. I deterred from confusing myself by not conjecturing why I held the feelings that I did, and instead enjoyed the moment that I was able to share; this moment that I hoped would never end. We walked and laughed and smiled, and the enjoyment of one another's voices brought balance to the pleasure of the arbitrary gazes of silence that we exchanged with one another. I could feel the warmth between us and I knew that she could feel it too. Everything seemed right, because it was right. I was right…No thinking, no ignorance, no doubt or worry.

Simply, love. I couldn't be wrong in my assertion...

We walked for quite some time, back and forth down the beach as the palm trees swayed and Californians began to make their way onto the beach, as parasites do to a stray dog.

"My nose is burning the fuck up. Goddamn," I muttered, rubbing it violently with my palm.

"The coke hounds nose is raw, huh?" Alexia asked jokingly.

"Shut up asshole," I jeered, irritated by the prickly feeling in my nasal cavity. I looked down and wiped tears from my eyes, nearly stumbling over a small rock the size of a baseball that protruded from the beach. I stared at it, disturbed that nature had suddenly made an attempt on my life. Intrigue rose as I ogled the rock, captivated by the way in which the water washed the rock as to not take it back into the ocean. It was beautiful. It was harmonious. It was love...I witnessed the soul of the universe; in the grains of sand, in the rock, in the washing water...I saw love and its connection to, through and from everything.

I am the ocean, moving freely over anywhere that I desire...subtle enough to fill a thimble and encompassing enough to plug an ocean basin. She is the sand, ever-present and vast. She is able to be molded and is still difficult to grasp. Our love was the rock, being washed by me and cradled by her.

"Why in the fuck did you beat that motherfucker with the baton, Melody?"

I had wanted to ask this question since we had retreated from the convenience store nearly three hours ago.

"Is it really that important?"

"Yes nigga! You robbed a gas station clerk of his car and beat him with a baton!"

Melody shook her head several times from left to right before jokingly reminding me of the rest of her criminal escapade. "I stole some juice too. Don't forget that..."

I could only smile at the woman and shake my head in response.

"Look, my father let him borrow that car when I was a child. He's my Godfather, the lying motherfucker," Melody said roughly. I could tell that she was becoming pissed just by talking about the situation. "My dad loaned him a ton of money a while ago. He chose to franchise a bunch of goddamned gas stations! Can you believe that shit?"

I shook my head in silence.

"Gas. Stations. The motherfucker ended up going bankrupt, faking his death and disappearing to California somewhere. My dad was never gonna search for him, they were raised together and that's some shit he couldn't do."

My face curled in disgust as I wondered why on earth any of this shit mattered.

"So he wants his daughter to do his dirty work?"

"No."

"So why on fucking earth did you do it?" My voice rose as I became irritated at her deflection.

She chose not to respond and instead looked left towards the sun, slowing her walk and abruptly turning around. I stood in place as she walked away from me, utterly confused as to what had just occurred. What had I said? Nearly in shock, I didn't take a step forward until Melody was nearly 20 yards away. I began a slow jog, caught up to her, and placed my right hand on her right shoulder. I leaned forward with my head turned towards Melody and began to inquire what I had said to cause her to become upset, when she looked at me with tears in her eyes. Her gorgeous face, the one that I was enamored with was streaked with mascara, its lines running from her eyes to her chin.

"What's wrong?" I asked as I wrapped my arm around her shoulders and placed her underneath me. She didn't bother answering, and buried her head into the side of my chest, bawling as a widow would who had lost her husband. Her clench around me was so tight that I could barely move. Her hug was like a vice grip, and five minutes passed before she had calmed enough to begin our trek back to the 67' Mustang, yet those five minutes felt like an eternity. I wanted nothing more than for Melody to feel better. I felt guilty for being adamant in my desire to understand why she did what she did. If I hadn't of pried, she would not have a reason to cry. I leaned away from her and gently grabbed the bottom of her chin, lifting her head so that she looked me in the eyes and spoke.

"You need a wet-wipe."

"Shut up," a bright smile rolled across Melody's face as she let out a hearty laugh, batting my chest with her hand in playfulness.

"It's just hard."

I didn't bother responding. She had talked more than enough

for the both of us. The walk back to the car was anything but boring; the silence of two individuals, with no need for speech to occur, is invigorating. We walked in silence for several minutes before anyone spoke.

"Do you ever wonder why they tell us that salt water is useless?" Melody looked up at me, her amber colored, almond shaped eyes shining even more brightly, and continued.

"I mean, our bodies are about 70% water plus our sweat and tears are salt infused. I mean, too much salt is horrible but as far as the ocean…I think that it's probably our greatest resource."

"Why do you think that?" I asked perplexed. What does she mean?

"Well, think about it. If water covers just about the same percentage of the earth in connection with the amount of water that makes up our bodies, then we have enough natural fuel to have as much fire as we want."

Numerous thoughts ran through my head as she spoke, and I genuinely had no clue what she was talking about. My face must have told it all.

"You can't be that simple, Sherm. It's so stupid that we overlook it."

"I don't know what the fuck you're talking about," I countered.

"What is the sun made of?" Melody asked in earnest.

"Mainly hydrogen," I replied.

"Exactly…what's the elemental form of water?"

"Hydrogen and oxygen," I replied. "What the fuck is this, science class?"

Melody giggled and smirked, "Yeah fucker, pay attention. Why on earth can't you burn water? Both of the elements are there, you just have to disconnect them."

"How would a regular ass person disconnect some fucking molecules?" I asked.

"Electrocute them," Melody said in an undoubted tone.

I was extremely intrigued by the knowledge that was being given to me, and wondered how on earth she knew the simplest forms of rocket science. She was a literal alchemist, if she could actually perform the feat of setting water on fire.

"I lived in San Francisco for three years in the People's Park. I survived, we all survived…on fresh fruit that was grown there. I dated a guy for a year and a half while I lived there, a squatter. His name was Hedlow. He used to work for the CIA but they like, gave him a bunch of acid and fucked his head up. He's lived in the park ever since."

My eyes squinted as I tried to envision a former rocket scientist living in a park, teaching other homeless people how to survive on their own. He was pretty much Jesus.

"So anyway," Melody continued, shaping invisible beakers and balloons with her hands as she spoke. "You're able to separate the molecules by attaching a metal rod to a battery and putting it into a glass of water. A few balloons to capture the gasses as they separate, a small container and small funnel…and you have a make shift torch. Simply light the end and let it burn."

"So why don't people do this shit?" I asked, a puzzled look on my face.

Melody's eyes rolled and shoulders shrugged. "Cause we'd rather pay for it."

My mouth dropped as the sensibility of such knowledge smacked me in the face as if it was a mac truck and I was a toddler. As it would seem, we as American citizens love to be labeled as consumers because we love to be endeared as vital sources of the economy.

"Why should you pay for something that is vital to your existence but is a natural resource?" Melody harped, her voice inflecting honest confusion. "People act like the only way for us to keep warm is through electricity. But hell, we believe that Ben Franklin captured electricity in a fucking mason jar FROM A KEY ON A STRING ATTACHED TO A FUCKING KITE!"

I laughed in amazement at the frustration Melody displayed. The way she tossed her hands high into the air made me think of a jubilant member of a Christian Baptist church expressing their praise for the Lord.

"Crazy thing is," I replied, "I've never even questioned that bullshit tale. It really doesn't make sense. Hell, that fat drunk motherfucker should have been electrocuted."

"A string bro, a fucking string! I could believe it more if they said silly putty but it is actually taught that lightning struck a kite and went down a piece of yarn."

"Good old Ben must have drunk a shitload of whisky," I laughed.

"Yeah and so did we as kids, believing that shit," Melody said.

We continued walking and laughing, content in one another's embrace while mocking Benjamin Franklin and the farce of our childhood educations. It's a baffling situation that a society can be in when they are taught the tall tale of Cristopher Columbus or that a fat drunk man captured electricity in a jar.

Melody and I's time together, however short it may have been, seemed to have lasted an eternity, and the daunting realization that it would soon come to an end increased to the point of pain as I thought of the possibility of never seeing her again. Don't think about it. Don't create it. At the frequency I've reached while on this spiritual excursion, anything that I think will come to fruition, whether I desire it or not. That is the beauty and the struggle of being connected to source energy. If you're not prepared, you may create something that you wish had never happened, even if everything else you wanted to put forth did. The manifestations of desires are dangerous...one has a desire to manifest, and this manifestation turns into desiring one's initial desire. As Alexia and I's relationship fizzled, I began to crave and long for a certain type of person. The person wasn't as important as what the person embodied, but when I held Melody and contemplated in the deepness of her eyes and the light of her smile, I felt the beauty of the surreal and the remarkable, and welcomed it. This love that I felt for Melody was an automatic resonance of our first encounter that occurred repeatedly...it mirrored itself.

"Where do we go from here?" I asked, looking into the future with reckless abandon. I knew that it wasn't a good idea, that the anxiety would inevitably come back to bite me in the ass, but the question parched the back of my throat and the only way to quench myself was to force it out of my mouth.

"Well, I guess we get in the car and go back to Vegas. You leave tomorrow, right?"

I took a deep breath and sighed. Was she this oblivious to the way that I felt about her? How often had she done this? Who was I to her? Was I just another guy that could sell weed? Or was she a hired gun? Hell, she was sent to keep tabs on me. Her father set me up with two imbecile's hell bent on dominating each and every fabric of my artistic integrity for their own god damned agendas. Goddamn it, I barely escaped having a bullet in my fucking brain. Pedro is a blessing. And, here I stand...with the woman of my dreams, desires, and thought's.

Melody leaned her head to the left and looked at me, her eyes wide and curious. She hesitated before speaking, stuttering a bit: "I'm really just not the type of person that you'd want in your life for more than a day."

"Well that's crazy," I retorted "Cause every day that I have seen you has been the best day of my life."

"History seems to be more perpetual than I thought," Melody replied.

"What the fuck is that supposed to mean?" I backed away from Melody, peeling her arms from around my torso. She took a step and reared back. Her eyes squinted and eyebrows bunched and for a moment I thought that she may punch me.

"Look kid, I'll give you a few wise words. I'm only here for the killer nights. Anything else, I'm not good for," Melody said. Her tone was coarse.

"Motherfucker...You know what," I turned and resumed the trek back to the vehicle. I didn't bother looking back, but I didn't have too. Maybe she does feel something. I walked until I felt her arm touch mine.

"You're a weirdo. You have tattoos and are afraid of commitment," I said.

"My tattoos still love me in the morning," Melody replied.

For everything I said, she had a response. And each time she responded, I was dumbfounded. Where had this woman come from?

Melody grabbed my hand, her soft and narrow fingers slipping perfectly in between mine. We walked the last 100 feet to the car in silence. By the time we reached the car it was 8:45 in the morning and the sun was bright in the sky. I hadn't noticed the change in temperature or even the loads of people that had begun to occupy the beach...my only concern was Melody.

"Dude I have 30 missed calls from Shelby and Corey. Fuck them. I'll see them shortly."

Between driving through the desert and walking along the beach, we both had neglected to remember that they were more than likely scared shitless that Melody and I had been disappeared, thinking that we had been kidnapped by the kooky elitist bandits from Friday night and thrown into a sewer.

"My phone is fine," Melody said. "No one is looking for me."

The expression on her face was that of desperation; sad and lonely.

I stared at her and wanted to alleviate the pain that she held inside of her, but she did a wonderful job of not letting her emotion affect her well-being in an outward way. She started the vehicle and slumped down into her seat.

"Look Sherman, I like you. We'll see each other again. Hell, you have a lot of pot to sell for me."

"Word," I replied.

"When's your flight leave?"

"6."

SUNDAY, 2:24 P.M. PST

"Dude we've been calling you all fucking day, we've got to go!" Corey screamed, jerking the car door open as Melody and I sat idled outside of the hotel.

It was hot outside; a sticky hot unfamiliar to Las Vegas. I could've felt that way due to the sand and dust that stuck to my unwashed skin from Melody and I's trip through the desert, but it wasn't that. It was the adrenaline. It seemed to flow from my inner being and escape through my skin. I felt its waves from the inside out. My blood boiled as I saw Shelby running behind Corey holding two duffel bags. As he raced forward, he ran into Corey as he climbed into the back of the vehicle, subsequently mushing my head between the seat and dashboard.

"What in the fuck is going on?" I asked, my face squished into a pucker.

"I think we fucked up bad, we fucked up real bad." Shelby mumbled as he sat in the seat.

Oh lord. How on earth could they have fucked up so quickly? And when? And the more pertinent question, how? Just as things were set on course, and Heaven was funneling into my body, the stark realization that Heaven and Hell weren't geological but things that solely exist in one's mind, sent chills down my spine. As much as I desired to meet, feel, and know Heaven, one would assume that I would have been able to will an encounter. Yet, as I have been afforded the opportunity to do so, I have also been afforded the opportunity to realize how stupid I really am. This isn't Heaven. This is Hell.

"What the fuck is going on guys?" Melody asked, her face scrunched as she stared in the rearview mirror at Shelby and Corey. The concern on her face emitted like radio waves, distorting the entire car's psyche. I turned and noticed the two nitwits ducked down, both of them raising their heads to glance out of the rear window like gophers.

"That shit that happened on Friday man, I don't know why we did that shit. The fucker Santi and his peons," Corey whispered as if someone were listening to our conversation.

I noticed that his face was more pale than usual. Sure, he looked like a vampire at times but Jesus, I'd never witnessed a white man so…white. What in the world had happened?

"Friday?" Melody and I both questioned in unison.

"Yeah man. You two motherfuckers left so abruptly all lovey dovey, hugged up" Shelby said.

I could hear the distress in his voice. A tension ran over my body as my mind raced. Why was my younger brother so distraught? I've never seen him as uneasy as right now. What the fuck did they do Friday? After I heard Melody sing, her and I left and did lord knows what. The night was a blur.

"Man, just drive. Melody, you know where Santi is? We really need his help."

"Yeah, Corey. But, what in the fuck happened? I'm not taking your ass any fucking where until you tell me what the fuck you all did."

"Melody, just fucking drive!" Shelby screamed with a red face, his eyes wide and glazed.

Two seconds later, the car jerked into drive, tires screeching as it sped from the hotel and onto Las Vegas Blvd. Melody cruised for quite a while, her eyes constantly glancing in the rearview mirror. Sitting in the passenger seat, I couldn't tell if she was looking for cops or at the two nuts in the backseat, snickering like squirrels. I didn't mind to turn and face them again, the road ahead required much more of my attention.

"We've got about a 45-minute drive fella's," Melody's voice was crisp and unwavering, quite the contrast to the two buffoons considered armed and dangerous due to purported criminal activity.

"You fucks going to spill the beans or do I have to drive you to the desert, tie your hands and feet and shoot the both of you twice in the stomach? I want to help you both, but if you're not going to fill me in on the foolishness then I'll just as soon kill you," Melody said in as even a tone as I've ever heard. It was almost sickening.

"Well god fucking damn," Shelby exasperated. "Quite the abrasive person ain't you? Look, take us to Santi. You don't need to know shit. Fucking flight attendant."

The steam practically spouted from her ears. Her face began to boil red with embarrassment and anger. Suddenly, we were idling in the middle of a Las Vegas Blvd turning lane. My head throbbing from smacking it on the dashboard.

"Fuck!" I screamed, looking at Melody while she shifted gears into park.

"Look you bitch ass niggas, I don't have the time nor patience to deal with the two of you. Fix your fucking attitude or…"

"You're the one with the attitude," mumbled Shelby.

Melody was irate. I assumed she would have calmed except Shelby just had to be himself and cut the woman off. What happened next I've only seen in movies.

As soon as Shelby ended his sentence, Melody was in the glove box, out of the car, and pulling him out of the backseat with a revolver in his face. Normally, this type of behavior wouldn't have caused one ripple to my natural essence of being a male that gives zero fucks, however it's broad fucking daylight in the middle of one of the most famous and heavily populated streets in the world! Who in the fuck does this woman think she is? Here I am, in the passenger seat of a vehicle that may or may not be stolen while a woman that I so desperately want to be with has a revolver to my younger sibling's head…a sibling that I will kill for, no questions asked. What am I to do? What would you do?

"Are you insane? You want me to protect you, yet you're being a little bitch. Get the fuck in the trunk!" Melody shouted as Shelby felt cold steel on the back of his head.

"It's your fault we're in this mess anyway. Why did you have to link him with my dad?" Melody asked, her voice fading. The frog in her throat turned her boisterous voice to a rasp.

"Melody," Shelby whispered.

"Don't Melody me! I had none of these intentions!"

"But…" Shelby said dimly.

"There are no but's."

Melody cocked the hammer and winced.

I hope she doesn't pull the trigger. I'll have to kill her. Lord. First, I'm an accomplice to an armed car-jacking and now I may have to kill a woman that I love. Is this Heaven? Have I found it in Las Vegas? If Melody had wanted me to see it so badly…If only I hadn't listened.

"Hey," I said nonchalantly, desperately attempting to divert Melody's attention from putting a bullet into my brother's brain.

"You can't kill my brother. Both of you get in the car and let's go. It's the middle of the day for Christ's sake. And I'd like to get to the fucking airport."

I expected Melody to disregard my words but to my surprise, she un-cocked the hammer, pulled Shelby up from the back of his shirt collar and pushed him towards the back seat. He got in quickly without uttering a word. I was confused. What should I do? Had I become too used to lunatics and nefarious situations? Nothing felt foreign. And for the first time in days, I was afraid because of it.

We rode in awkward silence for the trips remainder. I'm sure everyone wanted to speak but we were much too shell-shocked and weary of each other to do so. I can't trust any of these sadistic bastards. They're all out to kill me, I'm sure of it. But why? What happened? What had I done to deserve this? A few days ago I was sure of life. Eager. I thought I knew what I wanted. Now all I want is for the Feds to not pick me up while I'm putting two-day old pickled relish on an overcooked hotdog.

When this trip began, Shelby, Corey and I were fervent with energy to experience everything that Vegas had to offer and hopefully find Heaven in the process. Well, we found Heaven…and as of now there was nothing Heavenly about it.

We ended our journey in the middle of the desert, miles from Las Vegas, Nevada. The home that we pulled up to looked as if it should have been built in the African savanna. The scene was surreal: two ocelots, a cheetah, three Baboons and six Royal Peacocks roamed a 200-meter front yard that wasn't really a front yard at all; I felt like I was on a safari expedition. Three feet tall blades of Bermuda grass and whistling thorn covered the yard, and as we rode down a dirt driveway, a group of Rhesus monkeys hurled handfuls of shit at our vehicle from a lone Candelabra tree.

"Pretty shitty spot we're in, huh?" Corey jeered, staring out of the window while poo pelted his window. Even with the amount of tension in the car, we couldn't help but laugh at the irony of the situation; It was shitty. My nerves had calmed tremendously since my brother had almost gotten himself killed, and I assumed everyone else's had as well due our willingness to laugh at our shit filled situation. Maybe not though…maybe I was creating infidelity in order to conceal the sheer terror that I felt inside and all around me. Or maybe they were all at ease and I was the sole loser about to piss his pants. Hell, I had every right to be afraid…try traveling through an unknown desert with an armed robber and two murderers and see how you feel.

The long dusty path to Santi's turned to a pebbled drive that whipped left into a large circle that connected to the entrance path. To my surprise, no one was outside to greet us. I'm not sure why I expected a group of supporters to be standing like picket strikers outside of Santi's castle-like home, cheering and jumping from the ground. It would have been nice to have though.

"Well boys," Melody said as the vehicle careened to a slow halt in front of the walkway that lead to large double doors in the front of Santi's home. "This is as far as I'm going."

"So...you're...not getting out?" I hesitantly asked.

"This is Y'ALL'S stop."

"And so in the fuck what," I blurted, staring into Melody's mystic eyes as I opened the car door.

"Bring your fucking ass."

Melody winced with contempt, but I could care less. There is no way that she's not escorting me into this house. Fuck Shelby and Corey, they're grown. I'm the one with emotions as up and down as ocean waves.

~

"Nice of you all to stop by," Santiago said with his back to us as he sat crossed-legged on an oversized white leather couch. He held an open newspaper as network news blared from a 110-inch projector screen.

"I enjoy the news, but the shit that's going on in this hell-hole of a world is baffling to me."

As I pondered how he could read with the volume distastefully high, a headline ran across the screen that sent chills through my body.

Black Parishioners Shot Dead by White Male After Church Service. Who Is to Blame?

A few seconds later, a blonde haired man in his late 40's appeared on the screen. His white shirt shimmered under the bright production lights in contrast to his navy blue suit and red tie.

"God damn," Melody spouted. "He looks sick. I'm not listening to that shit. I'll be in the shower."

"Good, you need one." Santi retorted as he set his newspaper on his lap and turned to glare at Melody.

"Sorry I brought vodka to your bible study. Fuck off," Melody said, exiting the room.

I peeked around the corner that she went around and noticed a massive white spiral staircase that seemed to go 25 feet up. As she walked to the staircase with her back to me, the only thing that I could think about was what she felt like. Once she reached the steps and went around the first spiral her eyes caught mine, and the bright smile that she displayed during my insane acid trip days ago began to guide me towards her. I took about 15 steps before I heard Santi yelling from the other room.

"Sherm, you might want to get in here for this," his words snapping me out of the entranced state I was in. Melody kept her eyes and smile on me as she continued her walk up the staircase. I turned and began my walk back into the room with the others, however I couldn't take my eyes off of her and nearly tripped over a large white rug that lay in front of me. I have no idea how I managed to walk over the rug without noticing it, but the curse that Melody has me beneath could very well be identified as the culprit behind my obliviousness. Shelby and Corey sat on both sides of Santi when I entered the large living room, their attention absorbed by the words being spoken by the blonde haired man on the screen. I looked at the screen and Melody's words, "He looks sick," instantly ran through my head. Even though his suit shimmered in pristine fashion, his face did not. A visible angst hung on his face as he spoke about the death of four black church members in Georgia at the hands of a lone gunman as they walked out of a church service on this Sunday.

"I bet he wouldn't have gone to the hood and did that shit," Corey piped. "Why fuck with peaceful people?"

"The world is a shit place man" Shelby responded.

"I'm just saying. Even though the pastor might fuck the deacon's wives, the church people are still welcoming and loving. Especially the ones down south."

"I know. I know," Shelby shook his head and continued watching the screen.

"You don't expect things like this to happen in the year 2016," the news anchor said, his face wrinkling as if he was under duress. "I know that this may not sit well with the majority of American people, but this is not 1822! More young black men and women are being murdered by the hands of civilians and police officers, than ever before! Yes, the advent of social media has catalyzed our ability to view and become aware of injustice throughout the world...There is no place for this nonsense in America! Black people, Native people...why love a country that hates you? No other people on the planet would love a country and the people that run it if they were being treated as you all are. There is nothing that will guarantee the liberation of the black person from the culture that is oppressing and disenfranchising them. You all have pulled your pants up, went to school and graduated, yet innocent and unarmed black men and women are murdered, by police or civilian, at an alarming rate. Remember their names. They will ri...."

Suddenly the screen cut to a red block with white lettering that said:

We Will Return to Your
Regularly Scheduled Program Shortly

I envisioned television executives racing frantically to shut this man's diatribe on the murder of innocent black people down.

"He was really passionate," I spoke. Each of our eyes were still glued to the screen, hoping that wasn't the end of the anchors statements.

"His wife and five children are black," Santi said as he raised his newspaper back to his face. "I guess he has every reason to be passionate. Those are his kids that are dying."

"He could lose his job over that shit," Shelby iterated.

"Any other crazy shit going on in that newspaper?" I asked, stepping around the couch to take a seat next to Corey.

"Not necessarily. Some crap op-ed about The Big O and his stance on the American prison system. People really hate that guy for absolutely no reason. Hell, he came into office with over a trillion-dollar debt and got that shit down to peanuts. The guy is amazing," Santi said.

"Why do black people dislike him so much?" Corey asked, his face showing a concern that I had never saw before.

"That's a question we will never truly know the answer too," Shelby replied, an inane gaze on his face as he lazily scrolled though text messages in his phone. "Before The Big O, a lot of people, mainly the poor and the old, had to decide whether to purchase their medicine or their food. Now they…"

"Now they listen to idiot republicans and idiot democratic social engineers about a horrible economy and rising healthcare costs. Hell, the economy hasn't been better and the pharmaceutical companies are fucking booming…" Santi said, finishing off Shelby's statement better than Shelby could have done.

I noticed Corey sat with his hands around his mouth and his eyes squinted and I couldn't help but wonder what was on his mind.

"What you thinking Corey?" I asked as I nudged him with my left elbow in attempts to get something out of him.

"Genius's starve while the hacks get rich."

"What?" Shelby asked with a rumpled face. "What's that mean?"

Corey shook his head and sat up straight. He gazed at the white ceiling equipped with enough small ceiling lights to rival the stars in night sky of rural Kentucky.

"Black people have invented so many things for America. They've, hell, you motherfuckers, have done so much for the good ole boys of America, only for the majority to steal from and use you for your knowledge, expertise and wisdom."

"Well, aren't you so fucking insightful," I laughed, looking at Corey.

"No…Seriously," Corey retorted, his eyes wide and brows raised in concern. "That's one of the main problems with black people…You think everything is funny."

I looked at him with winced eyes, debating whether I should punch him in the mouth or hug him for being an honest friend.

"Not saying it in a fucked up way, but ya'll let white people get away with everything…."

Shelby leaned forward and opened his mouth in an attempt to retort but nothing came out. As I looked into his face I couldn't help but understand why he hadn't spoken. I couldn't lie to myself. Maybe Corey did have a point, maybe we did let people take everything from us. I often wonder about the transatlantic slave trade and the happenings of it. I often wonder about antiquity, from Plato to Hippocrates to 2 million years ago. Who taught the former? Where did they get their knowledge?

"It was a little more intricate than that," Santi chimed, his nose still in his newspaper. "No one truly understood warfare in the 15th century the way that whites did. In my opinion, they were extremely violent and virulent people…and still are today in many aspects. Ponder why and how a people were able to take hold and control the entire western world and essentially the earth. Violence. It's about fear."

"What about Genghis Khan?" I asked. I mean hell, that motherfucker was the bad ass of bad asses and was around 200 years prior. "He was a fucking maniac. You can't tell me that people didn't learn from him."

And that was the point in this conversation I suppose. People did learn, from everyone. They learned and adapted tactics and utilized critical thinking in order to form plots and schemes that were useful.

"Dude, white people ran away from white people and that's how America was basically created," Corey said with tight lips. I could tell that he wasn't very happy with the way that our conversation was heading.

"What does this have to do with a black president though?" I inquired, finally reconciling the conversation and where it derived from. "I mean, as a black president how could he ever rectify hundreds of years of slavery and nearly 150 years of systemic oppression?"

They each turned to look at me, and then reverted their eyes to the front of them, and stared off into space. Should I continue? I mean hell, I'm just as baffled as they are by this conversation. I'm ever more baffled about the state of affairs in the United States, however it is no surprise that they are too.

It seems that everyone dislikes The Big O and there is absolutely no reason to do so that I can fathom at this very moment in time. I mean hell, think about if you were The Big O, growing up in Hawaii smoking pot during the Carter presidency, and attending college and really enjoying weed during the Reagan era. I guarantee that you're noticing the influx of certain drugs within New York City as well as the changes that came to American government during the infamous War on Drugs. The intelligent conversations that you may have with peers and colleagues more than likely attribute to your position on the disparity of prison sentences between crack dealers and soft cocaine dealers, and you may have thought:

"How in the fuck can I jerk this shit around and create something more beneficial to everyone?" or even "When I get the chance, fucking watch! These people are going to flip their fucking shit!"

Think about the time in American history and realize that Ronald Reagan's system of economics has ingratiated itself into the American economy and culture over the last 30 years. With its acceptance came the flood of cheap narcotics; cocaine and heroin prices dropped, nasal medicine was sold en masse at an astronomical rate and the influx of manufactured drugs began to take hold.

"You fucked my people," Shelby blurted. "I'm sure that's exactly what he was thinking."

"Who the fuck are his people?" Corey questioned. Shelby leaned back into his seat, tilted his head and stared at the ceiling. Who are The Big O's people? Hell, he's a half Jew and went to grade school in Hawaii and Indonesia…. However, he's married to a black woman from the projects and has two black daughters…. shit, fuck it. He knows who his people are and so do we.

"Man," Shelby spouted, his eyes still gazing at the ceiling. "He's everyone's people. We all just need to embrace him. Hell, by the time he was running for office the military industrial complex that pretty much funded the second Bush was hedging bets on him anyway."

Corey was shocked at Shelby's statement.

"Fuck you mean? Hell naw, I don't find that shit possible," Said Corey.

"Why the fuck not?" Shelby asked, his eyebrows scrunched and face menacing Corey.

I thought for a minute that they may come to blows the way they were looking at one another. It would have been a sight to see however, I'm sure they both have an immense amount of energy to expend.

"I mean," Shelby shrugged his shoulders and began looking at the television again. "Maybe it's all a ploy…a big ookie doke."

"Possi…" I wavered, half of me wanting to wane the tension and the other half wanting to join the conversation. I couldn't even get the first word of my sentence out before Santi cut me off. As he began to speak he set his newspaper down and looked at each of us individually with concern in his eyes.

"No," Santi started. "Bush knew that he was getting a bunch of shit to his name but he never thought in a million years that a black Democrat would have what he has. Remember, Bush fucking took control of those god forsaken poppy fields in the Middle East and kind of treated the place like it was 'Nam."

"Kinda!?" I exasperated.

"Yeah but you can't really equate those two times because people now a days are functioning crack heads... like alcoholics," Shelby said.

He actually made a great point. The 1990's and 2000's ushered in a new wave of crackhead that functioned as productive members of society, similarly to the way alcoholics were and are. But that's not the point. And I suppose there is no point besides understanding why America is the way that it is and why the greatest president for the American people in the last 70 years is hated. It cannot be because he is black or that he is fucking up the economy. Be real. Unfilled jobs are at an all-time high so people can work if they'd like, gas is low so there's an illusion that more money is in people's pockets, and student loans can be forgiven. Fuck are people so upset? Its fucking Obamanomics.

But why do things seem so different now that The Big O is in office? Is it really because he is black or is it because he flipped some shit and got people to do what he wishes. This wouldn't be a bad thing if only the people that he got to do the ill ass shit actually wanted to do it from the bottom of their hearts.

"Yeah and The Big O relaxed those crack charges," Corey exclaimed. "When certain people started fucking up and getting arrested for heroin the government felt it was only right to change the laws."

Santi glanced at Corey with a fever in his eyes, and set his newspaper on the white coffee table sitting in front of him. His face grimaced as he hashed on Corey's statement. What the entire fuck is Santi thinking? I surely hope it wasn't too inflammatory. I'd hate to have to kick this old fucks ass in his own house.

"It had nothing to do with people getting arrested and everything to do with white people dying. It's common sense and a misnomer. If white people weren't dying no one would care," Santi murmured.

And it in fact was common sense. When black people were destroying themselves and their community with crack cocaine,

Reagan upped the ante that Nixon and Carter had created and bolstered. This prompted the change in sentencing guidelines which aided thousands of people, regardless of color.

"Seeing that the military industrial complex was and is right wing Christians," Santi continued as we gazed at him. "The argument that whatever the government was doing was a lucrative venture doesn't hold prudence until it's the other guy doing it. That other guy being The Big O. It's really the only way that you can justify the government profiteering off of drug money."

"It's basically got to be a black ops demonstration," I added. I was amazed at the insight that Santi provided, yet I couldn't bring myself to believe a word that he said. It was too far-fetched and too thought out.... but Santi must've felt my skepticism.

"When you create a culture as Reagan and Bush Sr. did that stigmatizes drugs, yet magically accepted all of them through various units, a person is going to find it difficult to revert the culture to a more pacified time," Santi explained.

"I guess you've got to have to have the foresight that people are going to be on roxy's, tabs, zanie bars and oxy's don't you?" The words came out of my mouth with confidence.

"Yep," Santi agreed. "And The Big O ookie doked the powers that be."

My brain was warped. All of the acid and cocaine and alcohol had finally gotten to me. What in the entire fuck were we talking about? What is the benefit of this and when the fuck am I going to the airport? My plane leaves in three hours.

"Oh snap," Shelby chimed. I glanced at him and winced my eyes, hoping that he would understand my expression pleading to tell Santi to get us the fuck out of here.

During Shelby, Santi, Corey and I's talk I had forgotten all about Melody. She hadn't been upstairs that long, but shit, I wonder what she looks like naked. I probably shouldn't leave the rest of the guys and try to find her though.... her dad might kill me.

"Even with Reaganomics, there was still a sell on the fact that there was an ookie doke happening. Like, Reagan ookie doke'd every...."

"What in the fuck is an ookie doke?" I blurted, cutting Shelby off mid-sentence.

"Who gives a fuck asshole" Shelby retorted.

"Yeah prick," Corey chided. "Just listen, you may learn a thing or two."

"I mean I'm just wondering what the ookie doke was because..."

Santi shook his head. "I mean shit, you can't understand that the Reagan administration knew that there would be a huge financial windfall? There was short-term gain for the middle class and the long-term gain went to the government. This basically destabilized the economy."

As Santi spoke, I couldn't help but wonder how this shit happened? How the fuck do we connect The Big O to the fuckery? I mean sure, we can compare the way The Big O talked about the resurgence of the economy with how Reagan spoke about it. We can even talk about the tactics they employed to keep citizens happy and more cash in their pockets...hell, who wouldn't want cheaper gas and affordable milk?

"Think about all of that fucking oil. The Middle East thought they could support our oil needs and that the situation would be mutually beneficial. Fuck that though, they couldn't keep up...they couldn't stick to the production demands that had been set," Santi continued.

"Didn't a lot of the land owners in the Middle East let outside companies take over their land?" I asked.

"Well shit," Santi thought aloud. His face frowned. "The Dutch, British...you know, those people...they kind of supplanted many of the original owners."

"Kind of like they did farming in America?" I asked.

"Basically" said Santi, his eyebrows raised and lips pursed tightly. "You own the land; I own the machine, therefore, I have the power."

Santi was right. It's been like that for more than likely thousands of years. You may have the land, but if I have the tools then I have the ability to harness your land for a benefit and then take your land from you due to the amount of cash I have accumulated based on my use of your land with my machinery. From farm land to oil, the tactics have stayed the same; money and violence. As the production of oil increased in the Middle East so too did the Middle East's desire for American currency. In addition, leaders were placated or ousted based on their desire to adhere to rules set by American government, and as the rules and terms of agreement changed, so too did the feelings of the Middle East towards the United States. Once upon a time many Middle Eastern countries were proud to be considered liberal, and utopias for women. Take Saudi Arabia for instance. Once upon a time it was a paradise, yet now it seems to be a hell hole for women and many others.

Shelby hadn't said much during our convoluted conversation, but when I looked at him I saw an intent and a curiosity surrounding events and circumstances from President Carter to The Big O.

"Is it true that once we sponsored the wrong leader or didn't follow directives closely," Shelby began, his eyes focused on the three of us. How on earth did he do that shit? It's pretty creepy, like one of those old ass paintings that look at you wherever you go.

"We'd get shut out and blamed?"

"Yeah, basically," Santi iterated. "People are whimsical and change their minds like the wind blows in different directions. We usually were blamed for the joy that people were having and how the Middle East was becoming more western. But hell, with the amount of cash they were making and the influence that the U.S. had on the Middle East during the time, what the fuck did they expect?"

"Fuck you, I want $200 a gallon type shit," I chimed

"Exactly! Fuck you, pay me. But shit, can you really be upset at that? Controlling oil prices was the biggest issue that Carter had, and remember this shit is mostly in Carter's regime...by the time Reagan's ass showed up things in the Middle East were shaky but this kook wanted the commies."

America had about enough of the rise and fall of oil and gasoline in America. I'm not old enough to fully describe the increase in the price of gasoline and oil off the top of my head, but I'm sure you can find this information out for yourself. It isn't imperative to my novel, so fuck it. Any who...

One of you favorite Presidents came in and said that the economy would get better and promised all Americans that it would. In order to have people perceive that the economy has risen, you can't have the fluctuation of gas prices hanging over your head. In order to change this, one must compromise themselves and attempt to support a kingdom of leadership that really hasn't gone so well. Bring in the country of mother fucking Nicaragua. President R knew that he couldn't really fuck with Colombians because they had too much money and too much power; the cartels were super powers. In order to combat these super cartels, the government began to seek and gain control of fringe nations. These nations were poor and desperately wanted American aid. In addition, many of these countries were in Central America and utilized as trade routes from Columbia to the U.S., with Nicaragua being one of them. One Presidents war on drugs became another's war on drugs, resulting in the devising of plans to patrol air and water surrounding entrance points into the U.S.

"We can't forget about old Bill...," Shelby sounded.

How in the fuck could we forget him? He sent more people to prison, regardless of race, creed, or nationality, than any other President due to his 1994 three-strikes bill. With well over a half a million individuals incarcerated during his terms, he single-handedly created the racial climate that exists today. The mandate that he enacted disproportionately sent black males to prison and created a cluster-fuck of issues that compounded with those of Reagan and Bush, and as a race, the black society as a whole has not recovered from it. Crack addicts have and still sit in prison for 20 years while heroin addicts get treatment for their "disease" over the counter. Still, one cannot help but feel that a step in the right direction was taken, regardless if it was The Big O, Congress, pharma corporations, or the boogeyman.

"Fuck no we can't forget old...", Santi began with ire before a seething Melody burst into the room.

There she stood, her chest and shoulders rising and falling viciously and a look intended to turn a person to stone stamped on her face, glaring at us as a mother would towards her child if they had forgotten to take the pot roast out of the freezer before heading off to school.

"The fuck's your problem?" Santi wondered, his face scrunched in amazement. The dynamic between this father and daughter is unlike anything that I have ever seen. They hate each other, this is for damn sure. Yet, this hate doesn't over-ride the obvious need that they have of one another.

"No motherfucker it's your problem. How the fuck did he fi...you know what, it doesn't matter... Fuck you, you probably told the son of a bitch."

"What the fuck are you talking about?" Santi questioned.

Shelby, Corey, and I sat on the couch looking back and forth, from Melody to Santi, wondering what in the hell was going on? Who was HE? And why was it a problem? Or rather, Santi's? As the two of them hurled curse words, I became dumbfounded at Melody…her movements, her language, her passion. I was entrenched in the harmony that her motions displayed; every gesture came from within and erupted. Each piece of her, from the white towel skillfully wrapped around her head to the one wrapped loosely around her body, held in place by her left forearm, moved as it should have. To be entangled in a world of mess was nothing that I had intended, but if it had to look like her, I don't think that I'd have it any other way. Was what I felt when I looked at her similar to what Heaven would feel like? Even though I was in Hell, was Heaven still nearby. What is Heaven even equal too? Is Heaven equivocal to sex? Or is it something more? As it stands, we can only equate Hell to being thrown into a raging fire…but what about Heaven? If Hell has a feeling and it can be described and compared to something, then Heaven must have a feeling as well. Heaven must feel like the best thing known to human kind, a sexual orgasm. If Hell is burning for eternity, Heaven is orgasming for eternity?

"Melody, I think that you're simply too many thoughts in a day. You can't keep up with your own shit."

"Fuck you, Santi. The bastard is almost here, you better figure this shit out or I'm killing someone." Melody stormed.

I snapped out of my maniacal daze as she turned around to run upstairs, nearly saddened that she was no longer in my immediate presence. What type of spell had she put on me? I've never felt this way for a woman, especially one that I barely know…it's more likely than not that I'll never see her again once we leave this place…. holy shit, how could I forget? What's going on?

SUNDAY, 6:18 PM PST

I'm unsure how to feel. Nothing like this has ever happened before. I'm alone. Weary. Weak. What has become of me? What has become of my life? In the beginning my sole desire was to find Heaven, and lord knows that I found it…and it found me, and everything that is part of me. Was the desire my downfall? Should I not have wanted this? As I stare out of the side window of Santi's helicopter, gliding through the air over deserted and treacherous land, I can't help but feel like the dirt beneath me; low, vapid, indigent. Nothing was as it seemed in Las Vegas and subsequently, Heaven was nothing that I had expected. Now, I can only sit and be thankful that I am able to uncover a bit more of myself in understanding; Make it an asset instead of dead weight. But what will it benefit me? Like I said, I am alone. Sure, Shelby and Corey and Santi are sitting here with me in the chopper…but the way that my life is set up…fuck them. I don't know how to feel. After everything that I have been through on this trip to secure the right to dominate Heaven when and how I feel, I'm still baffled at what to do next. All I'm left with is two nit wits, an old geezer, and a quarter million in poker chips. What the fuck is life? I came to Vegas lost in Alexia only to be blessed by the universe with a touch of fulfillment. Melody had provided something for me; a swelling in my chest happened when I thought of her. Everything that I yearned for, she gave. I found Heaven in her, as it was something that she in fact was. She felt like Heaven. To me, she was Heaven. And she is lost to me forever. Life has a funny way of making you realize that you are nothing but a shrivel of an ant's dick in the infinite number of universes that happen to exist. You are nothing. We are nothing, and life will take any and every chance it can to fuck you. I've never felt this way. Yes, I may be crazy… I had no clue about this girl, right? She was the cool ass flight attendant for Christ sake…the woman that I saw…and loved. I could blame the drugs on my abrupt and unforeseen emotions. It would be a plausible explanation to why my chest is eating itself with sadness and anger. I wanted to leave with more than poker chips…I wanted Melody. Her love. Her assurance.

Call me crazy…maybe I've never loved. Maybe I didn't love Melody. Maybe what I felt never happened. Maybe I missed what I should have had the entire time. Maybe I missed the point. Maybe I missed the signs. Maybe I missed the universe conspiring for me…. There will always be distractions…Did I give in to them too easily? Shamelessly? Maybe Alexia was the car I was supposed to buy. Or maybe Alexia was a test run…the longest and most passionate test run of my life. A test run that I would do over again and again, without hesitation. She was also the girl that I left in Las Vegas. The girl that I chose to leave in Las Vegas. The girl that I walked out on in Las Vegas. Why am I the way that I am? Was this what I was supposed to learn? Accept who you have and what you have with them, or be set to lose them? I have so many regrets. Why go towards Melody? Why want her? I went to Las Vegas and my soul will forever be there, and there is nothing that I can do for its return. What am I to do? The questions haunt me. I wanted too much in return for too little. I suppose in the grand scheme it's my own fault. I attempted to self-medicate by becoming subject to another person, enabling their power to consume and possess me. Instead of allowing myself to re-learn my Self, which was long forgotten in the wake of Hurricane Alexia, I latched onto a soul that didn't want to keep hold of me.

It was a lust, a beautifully constructed lust that happens only when the stars are aligned and God has granted grace onto one's crown. Tis the problem with lust however, that crown can swiftly be placed atop another's head. This is the destiny of many however, and many aren't worthy enough to wear the crown and be saved by that same grace. Pulled from a raging fire, I was saved…and I should be grateful. Still, I feel like I reshuffled my hand and ended up with a deuce of clubs. I've never really understood the saying, "Don't reshuffle your deck with a queen, and end up with a joker"….what the fuck is that supposed to even mean? Hell, if life is a game of spades, the joker wins every time. I wish that I could fucking reshuffle my deck and be awarded with a joker. I'd never reshuffle again. I'd have won at that point. I'd quit and leave the damn barbeque with my hand and never return.

Nonetheless, I suppose that I shan't fret on the past, as the now is the only thing that matters. My brother's marriage is going to be off, he and his best friend are fugitives from the law, and my heart is broken into 3,000 pieces. Our own actions have done us in.

And we're headed to Los Angeles, away from the chaos of Las Vegas. You're probably wondering how we ended up in Santi's helicopter...and that is a mishap within itself. It is disheartening that this opus is coming to an end, but to an end it must come, **until we land**. It isn't necessarily my fault, or their fault, or anyone else's fault that we're headed to Southern California. Shit hit the fan and we had to get the fuck out of dodge. Everything went haywire as soon as Melody ran upstairs. No electricity, police sirens and lights, and loud bangs and all types of shit that you only see in action movies. I was dumbfounded; perplexed. What in the hell was going on? Why on earth was law enforcement on a loudspeaker outside screaming for us?

"Santiago Mora, we know that you're housing those three fuckers! Tell them to come out with their hands up and I won't blow your fucking house up!"

It was an odd situation that we found ourselves in. I knew that something like this would happen, but I'll be damned if I go to anyone's jail or prison. I nearly began to panic at the thought of being caught up in a situation that could leave me with a ten-year prison sentence, but as I looked frantically at Shelby, Corey, and Santi, I slowly began to ease. If they weren't bugging out, then why should I? I'm sure that they had come up with a plan, and if not, fuck it, I guess we will all go down fighting...or getting shot.

"Come on, follow me," Santi spoke softly.

He didn't wait for us to respond as he walked out of the living room and into the kitchen. I hadn't bothered giving myself a tour, and I'm pissed that I didn't because the kitchen was even more amazing than the living room. Marble floors and marble countertops and gold accented appliances covered the entire room...Santi's real life was a movie.

As we paraded through, our reflections bouncing off of the softness of the floor and gold, I couldn't help but wonder why on earth the police didn't bust down the front door. I'm sure they had a search warrant with probable cause enough to tear the place down. As I pondered, Santi opened the right side of a large double door and motioned for us to enter quietly, placing his left finger to his mouth and waving us into the space with his right hand. It was a dark room and only lit due to the door being open. Once we were inside, the door was closed and a bright white glare struck each of our eyes. My hands went up to guard myself from the sight, along with Corey and Shelby's. What on earth was going on? I regained my bearing quickly, mostly due to being in a foreign and unbeknownst dwelling. When I opened my eyes, I saw nothing but a glowing soft white, as if we were inside of a cloud. The light seemed to have no beginning or end, yet if I stuck my hand towards an edge I reached it.

I reached my hand out and touched a wall. Its cold sent a chill down my spine. Are we underground? Above ground? Are we moving? Neither of us spoke to another, the sharp looks that we gave to each other were more than enough. Santi was the first and only person to break the silence. His speech was short, quickly re-immersed into the quiet, even though it cut through it so easily.

"That was Melody's husband. Fuck him. And Her. You don't need that."

I'm not sure how long we stood in that panic room…It couldn't have been more than 20 minutes although it felt much longer. Time goes slow when you realize nothing is or will ever be as it seems. I could think of nothing but questions that I wanted to ask Santi. Where is she? What is this? Why am I here? Who is HE? Life is taking me on a ride that I never wished to get on. I wanted to yell. I was in distress. The silence didn't help. Nothing did. Until Santi opened the door. The rest is a blur. I remember hearing a voice. "Run." And a strong gust of wind that turned the air around me into a storm.

~

"Yo," Santi said as he turned his head towards me. "Don't worry about the bullshit."

"How about you worry about flying," I reacted. Why would he tell me not to worry? This is bullshit. Look at the position I'm in…don't worry? Easier said than done.

"Your experience is the greatest occurrence."

My face scrunched as I stared at him, slightly disgusted that he would open his mouth to utter those words to me. This guy is insane. But, maybe he is right. No, he is right. It is right. Everything is right.

"Why?" I replied sarcastically. "Cause I'm close to God?"

"Cause you're close to Heaven."